BRICK BY BRICK

A Mathilda Holiday Novel

ANNA MCCLUSKEY

1

1.

Mattie's bright blue eyes turned a blank white as she shifted into seer mode to look past the peeling paint of the cheap motel room door. The apathetic young woman at the front desk had told them the room was empty, but it never hurt to double-check.

Actually, what the young woman had said was, "You sure? Nobody's staying in that room more'n a couple hours."

"Why's that?" Bernie had asked.

She had shrugged her skeletal shoulders, her eyes never leaving the computer screen in front of her. "Keep whining about a smell. Don't know what their problem is. This ain't the Ritz."

She'd typed something rapidly on the keyboard and given a small, satisfied-sounding grunt.

"Have you sent in the cleaning staff?" asked Sister Margaret.

"I am the cleaning staff," she'd responded dully, typing in another word and then frowning at the screen. "Can't find nothing out of the ordinary. Room 12's free, if you'd rather."

"No," Bernie had said, sharply. "We need Room 11."

She'd shrugged again and reached behind her, still staring at her screen as she located the key by feel and tossed it in their general direction. Sister Margaret had caught it.

Mattie had craned her neck to see what was so captivating. To her surprise, the screen showed a half-filled-in New York Times crossword puzzle. The Sunday edition, to boot.

"Check out's at 11. You get charged another night if you're still here."

But they had no intention of staying even one night in this dumpy motel.

Outside the room, Mattie held out her hand and Sister Margaret, whose eyes had also gone seer white, placed the key on her palm. This motel still used metal keys, and it was cold against Mattie's fingers as she slid it into the lock, jiggling it a little as it got stuck midway through.

Finally, she managed to get it in and turned and the door creaked open.

Mattie gagged as the smell hit her like a blast of dynamite. "Oh, that's not good," she gasped, covering her nose and turning away from the room.

Sister Margaret gently pushed Bernie away from the entrance. "You don't have to go in there, amigo," she said, softly. "I know the smell of a week-old body when it smacks me in the face, and you know there's really no one else it could be but Polly."

Bernie squared his shoulders. His lips flattened into a thin line and his hands glowed with a spell. He shook his head quickly, as though shaking it clear of cobwebs. "I have to see," he said. "She's – she was my wife."

Mattie nodded and her own hands glowed as she cast a hasty spell to close off her olfactory senses. The stench of rotting flesh abruptly ceased and she breathed a quiet sigh of relief.

"I guess the two of you are spelling your noses dull," said Sister Margaret, grimly.

"Want me to do the same for you?" asked Mattie.

Sister Margaret was a natural seer and, as far as Mattie knew, had never branched out into either of the other two disciplines of magery.

The warrior nun shook her head. "Someone has to sniff out where the fuck Shezza stashed her."

Sister Margaret shoved the door open the rest of the way and strode into the room, her head turning from side to side like a searchlight, her blank eyes peering around.

Mattie looked with her own seer sight, catching a glimpse of a slight shimmer around the sliding closet door. "There." She pointed. "There's a spell on that door."

"Good catch." Sister Margaret marched across the shabby room and grabbed the handle, jerking the door. It didn't budge. "Hmm. I can't tell if it's spelled shut or if it's just stuck and the spell is something else."

"I wonder if that idiot at the desk even bothered to get it open," Bernie muttered, making his own way over to the closet. He knelt to examine the track at the bottom of the door.

Mattie thought about that crossword puzzle. The girl might be apathetic, and customer service was clearly not her strong suit, but she was no idiot.

"Here we go," said Bernie. He pushed against the base of the door, forcing it back onto its track. "Should work now."

He stood up, and Sister Margaret slid the door aside.

She immediately reeled backward, a stream of vicious-sounding Spanish escaping her lips. The smell must have intensified.

"Yep. This is where it's coming from," she gasped.

Bernie stepped back, reluctance warring with determination on his face.

Mattie tugged on his arm, pulling him away from the door. "Hey," she said. "You don't have to be the one to find her."

She resolutely pushed back the memory of walking into her mother's hospital room when she was eighteen, the first in her family to see her dead, the first to know she'd passed.

Bernie shouldn't have to be the first to see his loved one's body.

Mattie and Sister Margaret moved forward together.

"Okay, now I'll take that damn spell," Sister Margaret murmured.

The glow around Mattie's hands pulsed as she extended her spell to cover her friend's nose as well.

"Thank you."

The two of them peered into the closet.

"The spell is in the corner, there." Mattie pointed, and Sister Margaret drew one of her swords, using the point of it to gingerly pick up a yellowed sheet.

Underneath it was another sheet.

"Screw it." Mattie crouched down, inching her way into the closet and poking the bedding. She shoved it aside and then the one underneath it as well. "It's just a pile of sheets."

"There has to be something in that corner," Sister Margaret frowned. "And we should be able to see it in seer mode."

"Unless it's yet another inscrutable piece of Auditor magery," said Bernie grimly.

The secret society they'd been fighting had proven to have more cards up its sleeve than the average mage seemed to know about.

Mattie shook her head. "Shezza would have no reason to use anything weird, no reason to be hiding the body from other mages."

Sister Margaret sheathed her sword. "That spell must be a decoy." She stood on her toes, looking at the shelf that ran the length of the closet. "There's another spell up here."

"Hold on a sec," said Bernie.

Mattie twisted around to see that he was grabbing a metal chair from beside the desk in the corner.

He set down the chair behind Sister Margaret and stepped back again.

"Thanks," said Sister Margaret. She climbed up onto the chair and looked at the shelf again, this time at face level. The corners of her mouth turned downward and she closed her eyes for a moment.

She must have found Polly.

Mattie turned away, a cold lump forming in her throat. She never knew the woman, not really. She only knew Shezza pretending to be Polly, but it must have been true to form to fool Bernie for several days.

And Mattie had liked the persona Shezza had put on.

"She's there," said Bernie. It wasn't a question.

"Yes," said Sister Margaret. "Mattie, will you help me get her down?"

Mattie nodded. "If I can see her, I can stitch her out to the van."

Sister Margaret stepped down off the chair and Mattie took her place. As soon as she saw the bloated, mottled-red body, her mind cleared and her veins filled with ice. The face was still recognizable as Polly's, and her throat was slit.

"It doesn't look like she suffered," said Mattie, her eyes roving over the corpse, looking for signs of any other wounds. "Just a quick slitting of the throat."

"Thank you," said Bernie, his voice choked.

Even so, Shezza would pay for this. Polly's only crime was throwing off the yoke of the cult that had brainwashed her, and Shezza's crimes just kept piling up.

Mattie pushed away the nagging thought that Shezza was also pretty brainwashed. Had she ever had a chance, growing up as the daughter of the leader of the organization?

"What would Ida do?" she muttered.

Ida Garaveldi, another victim of the Auditors.

No, not victim. Ida had never been a victim. She was another fallen soldier in this war.

And she would want Mattie to keep fighting.

Mattie moved her fingers in a complicated gesture, and Polly's body disappeared, stitched out to the van, as Mattie intended.

She jumped down off the chair. "Let's get the fuck out of here."

Tillie stood in the hallway and stared through the large window in the wall, a window that looked not toward the outside, but into a room.

Inside the room was a set of bunk beds, a cozy-looking loveseat, a small table with two wooden chairs, and, incongruously, a marble pillar with a woman chained to it.

Ordinarily, Tillie frowned on women being chained to pillars, but this woman deserved it.

She watched as a man dressed all in black except for a patch of white at his throat circled the pillar, stroking the woman's jaw line as he passed. "Now, Ms. Shezza–"

"Agent Shezza," the woman interrupted. She grinned at him. "Let's have a little respect, you shitlicking idiot. I'll refer to you by your proper title, Cardinal, and you'll refer to me by mine."

Cardinal Neubacher inclined his head regally. "Fair enough. You'll refer to me as Cardinal Neubacher, and I'll refer to you as a pathetic, slimy little weasel unfit to walk on God's green earth. How does that sound?"

Shezza grinned again. "That sounds like a fat load of bullshit."

Tillie frowned. Wasn't Cardinal Neubacher supposed to be some terrifying figure? A notorious tormentor of anyone who defied the Church? Someone whose name was spoken primarily in whispers?

Then the man stopped and looked into Shezza's face and an expression of pure compassion crossed over his own. "You have strayed, my dear. You have strayed so far from the way of true humanity."

Something in his voice made Tillie shiver. It was like a throwback to the Spanish Inquisition, where priests had tormented anyone they could get their hands on and pretended it was all in the name of mercy.

Shezza must have gotten a similar impression, because suddenly, she wasn't smiling anymore.

Her face turned hard and she spit at the Cardinal. "Even if I wanted to talk to you, I don't know anything," she declared.

Huh. She was returning to her old persona, the idiot sheep of an agent she'd pretended to be for years to infiltrate the group of rebels plotting against the Auditor organization. Tillie hadn't been expecting that.

Cardinal Neubacher took it in stride, however. He leaned forward and smiled sadly into the spy's eyes, and then kissed her gently on each cheek and then her forehead. He turned his back on her and winked at Tillie through the glass. "You'll talk, my dear," he said to Shezza, still looking at Tillie. "We start our real work tomorrow, and I promise you. You'll talk."

Tillie felt a hand on her shoulder and just about jumped out of her skin. Turning, she saw her best friend, Trevor, standing behind her, a wry eyebrow lifted.

"Are you okay?" he said, laughter rumbling just below his voice.

"Sorry." Tillie shook her head, a relieved chuckle escaping her own lips.

The door beside them opened and Cardinal Neubacher exited the cell, adjusting the cuffs of his long-sleeved black shirt. "Good morning," he said, pleasantly, nodding to them both.

"That was . . . very creepy in there," said Tillie.

"Excellent," said the Cardinal. "Creepy is just what we're going for." He leaned toward them. "You know we don't actually torture people anymore, right?"

Trevor nodded. "Sister Margaret told me that the Church has spent years building up your reputation so all you have to do is creep at people and they'll spill their guts, without having to actually, you know, spill their literal guts."

"Correct," said Cardinal Neubacher. He sighed. "To be honest, I'm not really sure why they decided I was the man for this job. But I suppose that's not for me to question." He glanced at the gold watch on his wrist. "I better go get ready for the service. I hope to see you both there?"

Tillie nodded. "Of course. Ida was. . . . We wouldn't miss her funeral for the world."

Cardinal Neubacher smiled compassionately, but after what she had just witnessed, it just came across as somewhat sinister.

Tillie shivered as the clergyman walked away.

"Listen, Tills, I want to talk to you about Mattie," said Trevor.

"Sure." Tillie nodded. Her sister's state of mind had been weighing on her as well, adding to her already considerable stress levels.

In the three days since Ida's death, Mattie had moved her stuff out of the small house she'd been living in with two of their former-Auditor-agent allies, and into an empty room at the convent. She'd been spending every waking hour training in either magery or combat, taking to a sword like she'd been born with one.

"It's like our parents' deaths all over again," Tillie said.

A few days after the twins' eighteenth birthday, their mother had died of cancer. It had hit Mattie hard, and their father harder. He had a heart attack and passed away a couple of months later.

And then Mattie had gone . . . cold. That was the only way Tillie could describe it.

She'd gone icy-cold and had zeroed in all of her focus on her schoolwork, determined to get the best grades, the best test scores, the best extracurriculars, and get into the best school and away from St. Louis.

She'd done it, too. She'd been class valedictorian, had her pick of Ivy League schools, gone to Harvard for one semester, and then had a nervous breakdown and spent two weeks in a psych ward.

After that, Mattie had evened herself out a little. She still wouldn't come back to St. Louis, but she moved across the country yet again, enrolling in the English program at the University of Washington in Seattle instead, and then heading to Portland for a graduate degree in something to do with education.

Tillie had gone in the other direction after their parents' death. She'd met a charming guy a few years older than her, dropped out of high school to marry him, and instantly regretted it. His charm quickly turned to gaslighting and emotional abuse, and she'd floundered, feeling abandoned by everyone in her life.

The only rock who had stuck around was Trevor.

Trevor was the one who had recognized what was happening and gently encouraged her to leave her husband. He was the one who had kept coming over, even after she'd tried to push him away, after her husband had tried to convince her that Trevor was bad for her, bad for them.

And Trevor was the one who had taken her to the hospital when her husband had pushed her down the stairs and broken her arm and several ribs. He was the one who had brought her divorce papers and told her it was time to ditch the asshole.

And she had. Her life had evened out after that too. She'd gotten her GED and enrolled in massage school. That's where she had discovered magery, and that's when she had begun to feel truly powerful again.

Tillie wondered if Mattie had ever managed to get to a point where she felt powerful, or if she was still blustering through life, the same scared teenager who had walked into a hospital room to find their mother dead in her bed.

Maybe she should have brought Mattie into the mage fold years ago.

She'd always felt that resentment about her sister leaving, though.

Tillie studied Trevor. She definitely should have brought Trevor in a long time ago. But she'd always been so protective of Trevor, and magery was dangerous. She hadn't known if he could handle it.

Turns out, he could, and she felt a pang of guilt about keeping him in the dark for so many years. Oh, well. The past was in the past, and all they could do now was look to the future and act accordingly.

As a seer, that's what she did best. Trevor, a natural stitcher, lived best in the past, noticing and recalling details of history and memory, while someone like Mattie, a natural speller, lived in the moment.

Out loud, she said, "We can't let her get that way again."

"I'm glad to hear you say that," said Trevor. He reached for her hand and squeezed it. "If the three of us band together, we'll be unstoppable."

2.

As Cardinal Neubacher stepped down from the altar at the front of the simple convent chapel, and people began to line up to receive communion, Mattie slipped out of her seat and headed discretely toward the back exit, wiping tears from her eyes.

She wasn't a religious person, and the Catholic Mass aspects of the funeral had been uncomfortable for her, but somehow Cardinal Neubacher's words about the comfort of a death well-earned had been moving anyway.

It was true – Ida and Polly had both died in service of a cause they believed in, and somehow that made their demise less futile. And then Bernie's eulogy for his wife and Ida's brother's tribute to her life as a mage warrior….

Warm salt water flowed from Mattie's eyes once again. She sniffed, then headed toward the cafeteria, hoping to help Sister Catherine set up for the wake before everyone descended upon the place.

Her footsteps echoed as she jogged down the stairs, her weeping under control at last. Keeping up her pace, Mattie ran down the hallway, sliding to a halt in front of the double doors to the cafeteria. She peeked in through the window in the door and saw Sister Catherine, the leader of the convent, bustling about inside.

Mattie pulled open the heavy door and the stout nun spun around, hands lifted in defense.

Lifting her own hands, palm out in surrender, Mattie grinned. "Don't stitch! It's just me!"

Sister Catherine lowered her arms with a rueful smile. "Sorry, dear. I'm a little on edge. What can I do for you?"

"I was actually thinking you might need some help," said Mattie. "They're winding things down up there; everyone will be here soon."

"That would be very nice, dear," said Sister Catherine. "Thank you." She turned back to the table she had been decorating. "If you wouldn't mind grabbing some more tablecloths, that would be a great help. They're on the center table in the kitchen."

"You bet!" Mattie hurried to do as instructed. She hesitated at the door to the kitchen. Closing her eyes, she pictured the table in the kitchen and then moved her hand to stitch whatever was on top of it into the main hall.

She grinned as a stack of black linens appeared in front of her. "Where do you want them?" she asked.

"That was very well done," said Sister Catherine, her voice warm and approving. "You're getting better. Did you even know what the cloths looked like?"

"Nope! I just pictured the table," said Mattie.

Sister Catherine strode toward her to examine the linens. "Well, that explains why you also brought in the cutting board that was sitting underneath them. Try to be more specific next time."

Mattie nodded. "Fair enough. Thank you for teaching me."

"It's my pleasure. Now go ahead and stitch these onto the tables. Every table needs one."

Lifting her hands again, Mattie concentrated on moving only one cloth onto each table, focusing on setting them down unfolded and centered on each surface. She could feel her energy draining, but each time she practiced, she got a little bit better at it.

And she needed to become a warrior worthy of following in Ida's footsteps.

Mattie thought back to Cardinal Neubacher's words.

"Some people are destined to make this world a better place, and that destiny lies in both their lives and their deaths. These two warriors did exactly that, through their strength, their sense of justice and honor, and through their willingness to sacrifice everything to the greater good. These two warriors lived lives we should all emulate, and they died the deaths that every warrior deserves. These were not the deaths of the ineffectual, of the wishy-washy, of the onlooker. These were truly the deaths of soldiers in the army of righteousness."

Mattie was determined to earn herself that same designation.

Tillie's eyes roamed over the crowd of mourners scattered throughout the cafeteria, quietly chatting. Her gaze landed on Giovani standing off to one side, his face shuttered, a clear plastic cup of red wine clutched tightly in his hand.

She made her way toward him, slowly enough to observe snatches of conversation as she moved between the clusters of people.

"--and I just don't know how much longer I can stick around here anymore."

"Do you remember the time Ida took down an entire coven of witches all on her own? They were raiding a–"

"She saved me, you know, when I lost my leg in the fight against–"

"--and that's why I loved her so much."

Tillie stepped up beside Giovani. "Your aunt was quite the woman."

He nodded. "I wish I'd appreciated her more when I was a kid."

Her lips twisting, Tillie shrugged. "I think she was probably the kind of person that a kid would be hard-pressed to appreciate."

Giovani laughed. "That's true. It was easier to see her merit as an adult, after I came back. I had so little time with her, though. And when I was a kid, she was so . . . strict. She was always teaching."

"And I'm sure you learned a lot."

His smile faded. "I just keep thinking about what the Cardinal said."

"Which part?"

"That she sacrificed herself; that we should all strive to be like her, a warrior, instead of an onlooker."

Tillie nodded, pursing her lips. "That struck a nerve with me too."

"I just feel–" Giovani burst out and then stopped, gripping his wine.

"Rebellious?" said Tillie. "Like you want to defy that definition of a life well-lived?"

He turned toward her, his eyes widening. "You too? I don't think that's the lesson we were meant to take away."

Tillie shook her head. "We were thrust into this. I never wanted to be a warrior."

"I wish I wasn't one," said Giovani. "Surely, those extremes aren't the only options."

The doors opened, and Tillie glanced over to see a trio of vaguely familiar people entering. A group of people near the entrance began exclaiming and gathered around the newcomers.

Tillie exchanged a puzzled glance with Giovani. "Who is that? I feel like I know them…."

Giovani nodded. "I recognize a couple of them. They're part of the rebel Auditor group, but all of them left after the battle at HQ."

Tillie's eyebrows shot up. "And now they're back? Do we think that's a good thing or bad?"

Giovani shrugged. "Let's go find out."

Mattie looked up from her conversation with Bernie, who was going on about some computer thing that honestly sounded very important, but made zero sense to her. A throng of people was assembling over by the door.

She jerked her head to Bernie and he broke off mid-sentence and followed her toward the commotion.

When she arrived at the edge of the cluster, Mattie saw Nicole, the leader of the group of former Auditor agents who were working with them to bring down the organization. She was making her way through the crowd toward the core group of newcomers.

Mattie positioned herself in Nicole's wake, following her into the center, ducking and dodging as excited mages turned and churned, flinging limbs all around.

Finally, Nicole stopped and Mattie stepped up beside her, joined just behind by Bernie, who had followed her in.

"Donna!" Nicole greeted one of the newcomers. "And Tom! Andrew! Are you back to join us again?"

"Not exactly," said Donna. "Sorry. We were hoping you could help us."

"Wait, let me guess," said Mattie. "You've been having weird dreams about the Pontiff and then your eyes go all black and you start attacking random people around you?"

"Well, not random people," said Andrew slowly. "We started attacking each other."

"We've been living together in an apartment in Boston," said Tom. "Because we all came from there originally, and it seemed prudent to ease back into our old lives, rather than just show up on our families' doorsteps."

"Of course!" said Bernie. "That's why the black-eye spell hasn't been affecting most of the ones who left. They weren't around other former agents. So, there was no one to attack."

"The black-eye spell?" said Donna. "So you know what this is."

"And more importantly, we know how to fix it," said Nicole. She looked around. "Can we get some teams of volunteers to sweep out their auras?"

Mattie raised her hand, and saw that others were doing the same all around her.

Nicole glanced around and pointed. "Okay, Tillie, Trevor, and Father Sean. You take care of Donna. Giovani, Amy, and Denise, take Tom. And Sister Regina, Christina, and Melissa, you're on Andrew."

Mattie lowered her hand.

Nicole turned to Bernie. "I hate to add to your load, Bernie, but–"

"No, please do," he said grimly. "I need the distraction."

She nodded. "Fair enough. Would you be able to put together some data for me? I need to know which of our agents are in groups like these guys, who might still be in danger from the black-eye spell. I know most of them went to their families, and are probably fine."

"I'll help you," said Mattie.

Bernie shook his head. "This is really a one-person job, Mattie. Thank you, though."

He spun on his heel and headed off, presumably to find a quiet corner to hunker down with his laptop.

All of the people around Mattie began to disperse as well, either to work or back to the celebration of Ida and Polly's lives.

Restless, she headed out too, making her way down the cinder-block-lined hallways of the school, toward the convent's training rooms. She'd never been one for working out, but some weapons drills would do her good right now.

3.

Trevor lowered his hands and nodded to Tillie and Father Sean. "I think that'll do it," he said. His voice was reedy and exhausted.

Tillie glanced at her smartwatch and realized they'd been working for hours – well past the time she usually ate dinner.

Donna's aura had been worse than anticipated, and Tillie wondered if Donna was somehow special, like Giovani, or if there was some other reason the black-eye spell had gotten its claws into her so deeply.

She had been under it longer, but only by a couple of days.

Tillie stood and extended a hand to Trevor to help him up as well.

He grasped it and pulled himself to his feet. He slung an arm over her shoulders, leaning on her.

Tillie's brow furrowed as she studied her best friend. His dark skin had taken on a slightly ashen hue, and there were puffy bags under his eyes. "Let's get some food in you," she said. "And then you're going to get some sleep."

"Am I all cured?" asked Donna.

"We think so," said Father Sean. "It's hard to know for sure, but this method seems like it's been working on the others."

"We haven't had anyone relapse after we've done this," Tillie added.

"Well, I really appreciate it," said Donna. She inhaled deeply. "I feel so guilty for leaving and now–"

"Don't feel bad," Trevor interrupted. "You have been through hell and back, and you deserve to be able to choose to take care of yourself for a change."

One corner of Donna's mouth turned up slightly. "That's easy to say, and it's certainly what I would say to someone else, but it's hard to apply to yourself without feeling like you've abandoned your friends and your entire cause."

"If it helps, we don't feel that way about you," said Father Sean gently. He leaned heavily against a chair and forced himself to his feet with visible effort. Once he was standing, he swayed, and Tillie rushed forward to catch him before he fell.

He smiled sadly at her and allowed her to help him lower himself back into his chair. "Thank you, dear. Any chance you could find me a cane? I know the sisters keep some around here somewhere."

Tillie nodded. "I'll be right back."

She strode out of the small ritual room they'd been using, glancing up and down the hallway, unsure which way to go.

A leather-armor-clad Sister Margaret emerged from the chamber across the hall and raised an eyebrow at her. "You look lost, chica," said the nun. She lowered the blue towel she'd been using to wipe sweat from her forehead.

Tillie ignored the spark of interest that always seemed to emerge from her subconscious whenever she saw the shapely figure of Sister Margaret. Even if she wasn't trying to focus on the whole taking-down-an-international-secret-society thing, she was pretty sure something horrible would happen to you if you hit on a nun.

"Is there a stash of canes somewhere around here? Father Sean is having trouble with his leg," she said instead.

"Yeah, sure," said Sister Margaret. She called back into the room she'd just left. "Hey, chica, you know the infirmary?"

Mattie emerged from the room, dressed in a sweat-soaked gray tank top and leather pants that matched Sister Margaret's. She held a water bottle in one hand and a small knife in the other.

Tillie's eyebrows shot up. Since when did Mattie voluntarily dress like these warrior types?

Her twin leaned against the door frame and casually holstered her dagger between her breasts. "I know where it is. Why? Is someone hurt?"

"Not hurt, exactly," said Tillie. "Father Sean overextended himself and is looking for a cane."

"Think you could stitch one out of the infirmary?" asked Sister Margaret.

Mattie shook her head. "I'm not familiar enough with the layout of the space…. Give me a second." Mattie moved her fingers and then disappeared, stitching herself out.

Sister Margaret smiled. "Your sister is turning into quite the mage in such a short amount of time." She nodded toward the sparring room they'd just come out of. "And quite the fighter too."

Tillie sighed. "Mattie has always been quick to pick things up. Especially when she gets all hyperfocused like this."

Sister Margaret's head tilted. "Hyperfocused?"

"Yes," said Tillie. "My sister has always been prone to fixating on something and devoting all her time and energy on that one thing for a while, until she burns herself out."

The warrior nun frowned. "We'll have to keep an eye on her, then, and make sure she doesn't push herself too hard."

Tillie was relieved to hear Sister Margaret say so. If anyone could keep her sister from working too hard, it was the nun who was overseeing her training.

Mattie stitched back in, a metal cane tucked under one arm. She held it out, and Tillie reached for it.

"Thanks," she said.

"Sure," said Mattie. She turned to Sister Margaret. "Thanks for the work-out. I better hit up the shower."

Without waiting for an answer, Mattie turned and jogged up the hallway.

Tillie lifted the cane and gave Sister Margaret a tight smile. "Thanks again." She turned and opened the door to the ritual room.

"–and that's it," said Father Sean. "That's how I lost my leg. All over a simple relic, I would have just given them if they'd asked."

"Witches," said Donna, thoughtfully. "Crazy. I always thought they were a myth."

"It just goes to show," said Trevor. "That enmity out of habit is always reprehensible."

Tillie walked over to Father Sean and presented the cane with a smile and a flourish.

He grinned back and accepted it with a regal nod of his head. "Why, thank you, noble lady."

Trevor cocked an eyebrow at Tillie. "Shall we grab some dinner and then I'll run you home?"

"Absolutely." She glanced at Donna and Father Sean. "Would you guys like to join us?"

"No, thank you," said Father Sean. "I really need to head home for some rest."

"And I need to connect with Tom and Andrew and talk about what our next move is going to be," said Donna.

Tillie and Trevor said their goodbyes to the others and headed toward the parking lot. As they walked in companionable silence down the hall, a door opened down the hall and Giovani and Amy exited a classroom together.

Tillie didn't know Amy very well – she was very introverted and tended to keep to herself for the most part – but she knew her as a powerful stitcher who had shown some real grit in helping to catch Shezza.

Amy was the one who had figured out how Shezza had released the courtiers from their cells by encapsulating them into books.

"Hey," Trevor called out to them. "We're getting some dinner; care to join us?"

Amy and Giovani turned toward them.

"Sure," said Amy. "We were planning to do the same anyway. The more the merrier."

"Is anything merry today?" said Tillie, wryly.

Amy shrugged with a small smile. "If not, there's nowhere to go but up."

The four of them trooped out to their cars; Tillie ended up riding with Giovani in his SUV, while the two stitchers drove their own vehicles, agreeing to meet at an Ethiopian restaurant on nearby South Grand Boulevard.

She kept the conversation light on the short trip, and Giovani seemed to be on the same page.

Between the funeral earlier in the day, the stress of what they were up against, and the weariness of an afternoon spent doing group magery, Tillie was just too exhausted to enmesh herself in any kind of serious discourse, at least until she'd had some food and some wine.

Giovani pulled into a parking space just half a block down from the restaurant and Tillie checked her watch. It was 7:05.

"Just late enough," she said. "No meter fee."

As they walked up the ramp to the eatery, Trevor jogged up beside them. A bell jingled as he opened the door and held it for Tillie, Giovani, and then Amy, who must have been right behind them.

Tillie was so tired, she hadn't even noticed the other woman there.

A smiling dark-complected man in his twenties greeted them and escorted the group to a table beside a tapestry-bedecked wall, placing a large laminated menu in front of each of them.

He turned to leave, but Trevor lifted a hand, forestalling him, and spoke rapidly to him in Amharic, the language his parents spoke, and a widely spoken language in Ethiopia.

The server beamed at him and asked a question.

Trevor turned to the group. "How does a bottle of tej sound? It's an Ethiopian honey wine."

"Sounds fantastic," said Amy.

"You know I'm always in," agreed Tillie.

Giovani nodded as well.

Trevor spoke to the server again, and he hurried off.

"Well," said Amy, opening her menu and then closing it again immediately. "I've never had Ethiopian food, and you seem pretty plugged in, so I'm going to go ahead and let you order me whatever you recommend."

"Ethiopian food is generally served family-style," said Trevor. "So, if you'd like, I'll just order a few dishes for the table and they'll bring it out on a big tray of injera."

Amy gave him a blank look.

"It's a fermented flatbread," said Tillie. "It's really delicious."

"Cool," said Amy. "I'm in."

"As long as it includes some beyainatu," agreed Tillie.

"Why not?" said Giovani. "Weird food will get my mind off of how overwhelmed I feel."

Trevor lifted his eyebrows. "My culture is 'weird' to you?"

Giovani shook his head vigorously. "No, no, I'm sorry, I didn't mean–" He broke off as he looked at Trevor's widening smile. "Oh, you're fucking with me."

Just then their server returned with four glasses and a bulb-shaped decanter filled with an amber liquid. He poured them each a serving and left the bottle in the middle of the table.

Trevor ordered their dinner and Tillie added a request – in English – for water as well.

The server smiled, nodded, and hurried away.

"Cheers," said Amy, lifting her glass.

Tillie raised hers as well. "To Ida Garaveldi."

"May her spirit live on in each of us," added Trevor.

"And possess us in battle and at tea-time," finished Giovani.

The four of them clinked glasses and sipped their wine.

Tillie savored the sweet, slightly alcoholic flavor. It always reminded her of orange juice.

"This is wonderful," said Amy. She took another sip. "It almost makes you forget that you've spent the past several years brainwashed by a secret society you've now sworn to dismantle with no idea of how to do it and have just realized that you've only scratched the surface of what crazy magics they're capable of."

Tillie noticed a startled glance from a teenage girl sitting with her family at a nearby table.

She gestured to Amy to lower her voice; she was too tired to put up a sound shield, and besides, it was dim in the restaurant and people would be bound to notice if her hands started glowing.

"Almost," replied Giovani. "Not quite, though."

"There has to be a way to find out," said Trevor. "We don't stand a chance if we're fighting blind."

"Well," said Giovani. "We know what agents know. What we don't know is what the court knows."

"You know what agents know," Tillie pointed out. "I have no idea, and neither do the nuns or priests."

"And I don't even know what all you regular mages know," said Trevor. "It's frustrating as hell, to be honest, being tossed into something this intense as a novice."

Tillie felt another pang of guilt. That was her fault. Both that he had only just found out, and that he had found out at all.

She should have either kept him out of it entirely by playing it safer, or brought him in years ago.

Well, it was too late now. No sense in dwelling on the past.

Tillie reached out and squeezed his hand in a silent apology anyway.

Trevor glanced at her and smiled slightly, giving her a small nod, as though he understood exactly what she was trying to say. He probably did – they'd always had that kind of connection, ever since they were kids.

And still she'd kept this terrible secret from him.

With an almost tangible effort, Tillie pulled herself up out of the guilt spiral she was starting to descend back down. This was the downside of all the stitching she'd been doing lately – she was no longer living primarily in the future. The past and present were intruding more and more on her psyche, and it was very confusing.

She turned her attention back to the conversation at the table, taking another sip of honey wine.

"–a committee to do exactly that," Giovani was saying. "With one of each discipline from the Auditors and one of each from the non-Auditors to help the entire group get on the same page."

"And the court magics?" asked Trevor. "How are we going to find out about those and get them integrated into the whole?"

"I have a thought," Amy ventured. She stopped, as though waiting for permission to continue.

Trevor gave her an encouraging nod.

"What about the books from the HQ stations?" she said. "I was assigned to a couple of different HQ's, and they all have libraries. Some of those libraries were more secluded than others, and there were a few of them where agents were subtly discouraged from entering, except for the station agents, I mean. The ones who were supposed to be taking care of the rooms. I even noticed a few times that I physically couldn't grab some books."

Tillie frowned. "You mean they were affixed to the shelves or something?"

Amy shook her head. "No, I mean I couldn't bring myself to pull them down. I could reach toward them to dust the shelves, but anytime I got curious and wanted to grab them to flip through, I found myself turning away to browse a different shelf instead."

"Fascinating," said Trevor. "Only certain books?"

Amy nodded.

"We should start with those," said Giovani. "Do you remember if they were in any particular location?"

"There were some in every HQ I went to," she said. "But I remember more than usual in this weird super-secure station out in the middle of nowhere Utah."

Tillie sighed. Utah was a bit far to be stitching things in from, especially if only Amy knew where and what they were.

"That's going to be tricky." Giovani echoed her thoughts. "I've never even been to that station."

"That's the station I was at when I came over to the dark side," said Amy. "So, there are actually a couple of people in our group who were stationed there with me at the same time. Paul, in particular, is a strong stitcher who should be able to help."

Tillie glanced up and saw their server approaching with a large round tray. She perked up. Food was coming.

The man set down a big plate in the middle of the table. The plate was lined with the spongy flatbread called injera, and mounds of various colorful, sauce-covered foods were arranged throughout.

He set down a pitcher of water and four stacked tumblers as well, and a small plate with extra injera.

Trevor thanked him and he left.

Tillie and Trevor showed Giovani and Amy how to tear off pieces of injera and scoop up the meal with the bread, and the group dug in, leaving aside the discussion of magery and intelligence-gathering in favor of physical nourishment.

4.

Mattie dodged as a huge object flew directly at her head.

"No," admonished Sister Catherine. "Don't dodge it; stitch it away." She threw another giant foam "rock."

"But in battle, I'll be using everything at my disposal, right?" Mattie protested. Nevertheless, she stitched the new one to a spot directly over Sister Catherine's head, dropping it onto her teacher. "So, why can't I dodge or put up a shield?"

"Because today we're practicing stitching," Sister Catherine responded, throwing two more of the training rocks at once.

Mattie stitched one away, but the other hit her squarely in the face. "Ugh. How do the fuzzy bits always manage to get into my mouth?" she sputtered.

Sister Catherine grinned and threw another one. "We make them special so they'll do that."

Focusing on the rocks, Mattie stitched three more into various points in the room, trying to get as many back toward her opponent as possible, but as they began coming faster and faster, mostly just managing to get them anywhere away from her.

"Picture this," Sister Catherine lectured as she bombarded Mattie mercilessly. "You're facing a trio of mages. There's a speller who has most of your body in stasis, but you've managed to free your fingers and you've got a shield around them stopping her from freezing them again. There's a stitcher who is tossing rocks at you, and a seer who is predicting your dodges and feeding that info to the stitcher. So dodging doesn't do any good. All you can do until back-up arrives is stitch the rocks away from yourself."

"Why am I not throwing spells at them, then?" Mattie demanded, stitching three more rocks back toward Sister Catherine. In the spirit of this new exercise, she froze the rest of her body, using only her hands to ward off the rocks.

"All of your energy is focused on keeping the rocks away," said Sister Catherine.

"Then I would put up a shield to keep them out," Mattie objected. "The only reason I know not to use a shield in battle is because my own offensive magics wouldn't go through it. But if I can't use lightning or fireballs anyway, why not a shield?"

"Because," Sister Catherine paused. "Hmm."

"In fact," Mattie formed a spell in her mind and then combined it with a stitch, forming a very special shield. "Hit me again."

Sister Catherine tossed a rock toward Mattie's shield, and the stitch she had just combined it with grabbed onto the rock as it hit the shield. The rock disappeared and blinked back in over Sister Catherine's head.

Sister Catherine stepped to the side, neatly dodging it as it fell, and applauded. "Very good! I've never seen anyone do that before. Where did you learn it?"

Mattie shrugged, grinning. "I just thought of it."

"Very impressive, dear. Let's see how long you can keep it up." The silver-haired nun tossed three more rocks toward Mattie's new shield.

Mattie got her hands moving just in time, managing to insert two stitches into the shield. The third rock bounced off the shield and tumbled to the floor.

Just then, a knock sounded on the door to the training room.

Sister Catherine held up her hands to Mattie, signaling a pause in the exercise. "Come in," she called.

The door opened just wide enough for Cardinal Neubacher to poke his head in.

Mattie shivered. Inspiring as his eulogy had been, up close, the guy gave her the creeps. Something about his bland smile and cold eyes…. She supposed that's why he was so good at his job, but he didn't seem able to turn off the torturer vibe.

"Am I interrupting anything?" he asked, his voice mild.

Mattie sighed. Obviously he was interrupting something. There was even a sign on the door that said that training was in progress. If something is in progress, then knocking on the door and poking your head in is always interrupting.

She kept her mouth shut, however, and instead practiced stitching a foam rock from one side of the room to the other and back, over and over, as she listened to Sister Catherine converse with the creepy Cardinal.

"We're about ready for a break anyway," said Sister Catherine warmly. "What can I do for you?"

"It's this Agent Shezza person," said Cardinal Neubacher.

"She's proving to be a tough nut to crack, isn't she?" said Sister Catherine.

"Shezza is very intelligent," Cardinal Neubacher agreed. "Very crafty, wily, and obviously well-trained in a variety of espionage-related tactics, including withstanding torture. Not that I'm actually torturing her, but I suspect she may figure out that particular ploy soon."

"Oh, dear," said Sister Catherine. "I'm afraid I don't know what to tell you about that; it's really not my area of expertise."

Cardinal Neubacher's thin lips tightened in a small smile that should have looked benevolent but really, really didn't on his face. "It is my area of expertise," he said gently. "She seems very comfortable where she is, and this gives her a bit of an advantage. I feel if I have full access to my own tools and my home ground, I will be able to extract the information we need."

"You can't just take her away!" Mattie burst out. She glared at the Cardinal. "We need the information she has. If you take her to the Vatican, how do we know that anything you get out of her will even come back here at all?"

Cardinal Neubacher's cold, dead eyes turned on Mattie as he studied her for a moment before responding. "In this age of the world wide web, it is very easy to share information, even between such vast distances as between Vatican City and the United States."

Mattie crossed her arms, refusing to be intimidated. Okay, at least refusing to show she was intimidated. "I didn't say it wasn't easy. I said you might not do it."

"I see." Cardinal Neubacher's lips twitched in a particularly condescending way, and Mattie's eyes narrowed.

Sister Catherine stepped in between them before Mattie could respond. "Let's remember, please, that we're all on the same team here."

Mattie glowered, but said nothing; she respected Sister Catherine and this was her home.

Cardinal Neubacher nodded courteously to the nun. "I would like to take her, Sister, but this is your fight, and I'll abide by your decision."

Sister Catherine chewed on her lip for a moment before speaking. "Please understand, Cardinal, that I do not share

Mattie's distrust. I know you, I trust you, and I trust our superiors in the Church. But nevertheless, I would also prefer to keep her here under our roof. This is a secure facility; our order has always been accustomed to keeping dangerous prisoners here, and it's well-fortified. Additionally, this is a volatile situation, and at this point it's more about ensuring that any necessary information is extracted and analyzed here immediately, rather than far off, where it might take precious time to reach the ears of those who need it."

Cardinal Neubacher nodded again. "Fair enough, Sister. I will continue to work on the detainee in your care."

He glanced at Mattie and she smirked at him.

The Cardinal frowned back at her, his face growing extra sinister before he spun on his heel and exited the room.

Sister Catherine placed a gentle hand on Mattie's shoulder. "I know you feel like you've won something, dear, but that man is not an enemy you should be glad to have."

Mattie shrugged. "I thought he was just a pretend torturer, right?"

"Sure," said Sister Catherine. "But he's a real Cardinal, and very highly placed."

"I'm not Catholic," said Mattie.

"The Church has fingers in more pies than you might imagine," said Sister Catherine. "I don't think the world as a whole knows how much power it still has. It might feel like the era of the Pope ruling the world has passed, but it's still closer to true than you know. And Cardinal Neubacher is very close to the ear of the Pope."

Mattie stared at the nun. "So, what? I'm supposed to just kowtow to the creep, cower in fear? You stood up to him."

Sister Catherine smiled slightly. "I can afford to. You have a little less power. And I might not always be around to lend you my clout."

Mattie pressed her lips together, and Sister Catherine sighed.

"You're a free woman, of course," said the sister. "And you'll do as you please. Just keep what I've said in mind next time you tangle with Cardinals. Now, if you don't mind, I believe I've reached the end of my teaching energy for the evening."

Mattie nodded. "Sure. Thank you for your time, Sister." She paused. "And for the warning."

Sister Catherine gave Mattie's shoulder a small squeeze and then she left the room.

5.

Tillie jogged up the stairs to her second-floor condo, feeling somewhat refreshed and quite motivated by the conversation at dinner, and then the long discussion she and Trevor had had outside in his car.

The group had made some solid plans for sneaking into some nearby Auditor HQs to steal books, and had even talked about the possibility of infiltrating the station in Utah that Amy had said seemed to be of oddly high importance.

She looked forward to bringing their plans to the rest of the group the next day, and for the first time since Ida Garaveldi's death, Tillie found herself feeling hopeful.

She frowned. Chatting with Trevor hadn't been as good. There was a strain over their relationship – had been ever since she'd run off and Trevor had found out about her years-long deception.

Tillie shoved her guilt away – again. She resolved to clear the air next chance she got. This festering wasn't good, and their friendship meant too much for her to let a mere complete overhaul of reality get in the way of it.

As she finally turned the corner to the hallway that contained her condo, Tillie was startled to find Giovani leaning against the wall beside her front door.

He pushed himself upright as she approached and gave her a nervous smile, running his hands through his sandy hair. "Hi."

She smiled back, genuinely glad to see him, if a little confused by it. "Hello, stranger. I feel like I just keep running into you."

"Yes. Sorry." He shoved his hands into the pockets of his black pants. "I hope this doesn't give off too stalker-ish of a vibe."

"Vibe?" Tillie raised an eyebrow as she unlocked her door. "You've been hanging around my sister too much. You're starting to sound distinctly slangy."

Giovani laughed. "That's probably true. It's funny how one tends to pick up bad habits from one's co-conspirators."

"Anyway," Tillie continued. "You're always welcome here. I hope I've made that clear."

"Thank you." Giovani followed her into the living room and sat down on what was becoming his habitual spot on her emerald-green sofa. "I just– My house feels so empty since Aaron left."

"Aaron left?" Tillie blinked at Giovani. Aaron had been one of their most passionate members; Tillie had considered him to be one of the leaders of their little movement, in fact.

He and Giovani had rented a small house near Trevor's in the aftermath of the battle at the St. Louis HQ, and he had seemed very dedicated to the cause.

Giovani nodded. "That black-eye spell was really hard on him. He's kind of a control freak, and the way it took over just kind of pushed him toward the breaking point. And he was close to Polly and Bernie; Polly's death was the last straw."

Tillie nodded. "That's fair. Not everyone is cut out to be a revolutionary. Still, that one surprises me. You can stay here for the foreseeable future. Consider my spare room yours."

"I really appreciate that," he said.

Tillie sat down and crossed her legs. Then she uncrossed them. She could feel the silence stretching toward awkwardness, so she instinctively said the only words always guaranteed to diffuse such things: "Shall I make us some tea?"

Mattie stormed through the halls of the convent, feeling more frustrated with every second, and wishing her tiny suite wasn't so far away from the training rooms. On the other hand, the walk was definitely helping to diffuse her furious energy.

The nerve of that creepy-ass Cardinal! Trying to snatch away their best asset and take her to the Vatican, where she would probably disappear into a warren of catacombs and never be heard from again.

Any information extracted from the spy would be diluted by the time it made its way back here, if it ever did at all. Plus, Mattie didn't trust him not to resort to actual torture, far from the watchful and compassionate eyes of the good Sisters of Saint Joan.

And while she had no illusions that Shezza wouldn't hesitate to torture any one of them, that didn't mean stooping to such levels was appropriate. Plus, she had seen numerous documentaries that demonstrated that torture was not just inhumane, but ineffective as well.

Really, why were they even entrusting Shezza to Cardinal Neubacher to begin with? Making her think she was going to be tortured was actually a form of torture, right? To say nothing of keeping her chained up in that cell.

The woman was brainwashed and they should be using anti-brainwashing techniques; making her understand that she was on the wrong side, and convincing her to switch over to theirs. Then she would spill everything.

Of course, that took time, didn't it?

One of the most frustrating aspects of this whole operation was that Mattie and her friends had no idea what the Pontiff was doing, and how much time they might actually have to plan their next step. They also had no idea what their next step should be or how to achieve their eventual goal of taking down the organization.

Mattie's rage was quickly fading into hopelessness, when she turned a corner and smacked right into Sister Margaret.

Her breath whooshed out of her as the hilt of one of her friend's twin swords poked her in the belly.

Mattie scrambled to keep her balance, aided by Sister Margaret's quick reflexes as she grabbed her arms and steadied her.

"Sorry about that," said Sister Margaret, her cheery voice countering Mattie's mood. "You okay?"

"Yeah, I think so," Mattie gasped.

"You sure were traveling fast," Sister Margaret observed. "Where were you going in such a hurry?"

"Just back to my room," said Mattie. "I wasn't so much in a hurry as I was pushing forward, fueled by righteous wrath."

"Uh oh." Sister Margaret's eyebrows shot up. "Anything I can help with?"

Mattie paused, studying the warrior nun. She glanced around to make sure they were alone and then took a couple of steps to sit down on a bench situated against the wall. "What made you want to become a nun?"

Sister Margaret raised her dark eyebrows even further, pushing them halfway up her forehead. "That's a complicated question with a lot of different answers, depending on the angle. Can I have a little bit of context, amiga?"

Mattie sighed. "I'd rather not, to be honest. But I see what you mean." She slumped against the back of the bench. "I hate complicated things. I want everything to be cut and dried, black and white, simple. And nothing – literally nothing – seems to work that way these days."

Sister Margaret sat down beside her, somehow managing to do so gracefully, in spite of her swords.

How the hell did she do that?

Mattie forced herself to focus on the conversation.

"These days?" said Sister Margaret. "Was there ever a time when it worked that way?"

"No," Mattie admitted. "But it's worse now. It's worse with magic and secret societies and back here with Tillie."

"What's Tillie got to do with it?" asked Sister Margaret.

Mattie's lips twisted as she thought through her response. Why were things always so complicated with Tillie? It wasn't so bad when they were two thousand miles apart and just texting all the time. "I love Tillie," she said. "I do. She's my sister. My twin sister, no less. But love and sisterhood gets all mixed up with envy and resentment." She paused. "Tillie and I are identical, but she's always been considered the pretty one, and I'm the nerdy one. And everything always seems to come so easily to her. She's got money and she always has lots of friends and she just lives this frivolous life–"

"I don't think that money came easily," interrupted Sister Margaret. "The life of a sex worker might look very glamorous, especially the way Tillie presents herself, but I can see a lot of trauma in her."

Mattie blinked. It hadn't really occurred to her that Tillie had ever been traumatized. She just seemed to take everything in stride.

"How well do you really know your sister?" said Sister Margaret, gently. "How much time have you two spent together as adults?"

Sighing, Mattie scrubbed her face in her hands. "Probably not enough," she admitted. "Something to rectify now that I'm back in town."

"Good." Sister Margaret nodded her approval.

"It's not just Tillie, though," said Mattie. "I keep forgetting that I also am supposed to be working out my divorce in Oregon right now – my court date is approaching quickly – and my old boss keeps leaving me these voicemails and emails asking me to come back and wondering if I know where her boss is–"

"That's the boss who turned out to be a spy for the Auditors, right?" Sister Margaret interrupted.

"Yeah."

"Okay, well, I gotta say, since you brought it up," said Sister Margaret, "one reason I took vows was because it helped make things simpler."

Mattie cocked her head. "How so?"

"I have to make very few decisions on behalf of myself," said Sister Margaret with a small laugh. "I make decisions on behalf of the order or at the behest of Sister Catherine or Mother Elizabeth out at our other convent in Springfield. Or I act upon decisions made by my superiors. But I don't have to worry about what I need to do for me. That decision is already made."

"Huh." Mattie pondered this and then nodded slowly. "That makes sense. But what if you disagree with decisions that have been made on your behalf?"

"I have faith that those decisions are backed by my Lord," said Sister Margaret, touching the crucifix that hung on a chain around her neck, gold against the deep brown of the leather armor she always wore.

"Huh," said Mattie again. "That's where it all falls apart for me. Sorry," she added.

Sister Margaret grinned. "You don't have to be sorry just because you don't share my faith. I understand that it's unusual and it certainly can't be forced. Nor should it be."

"Okay, thanks," said Mattie. She was still struggling to put into words the questions she really wanted to ask. Sister Margaret seemed to have so much more figured out than she did, and right now she really needed to figure something, anything, out.

Tillie sat down across from Giovani and poured the tea – herbal, in deference to the late hour. "So, we lost Aaron," Tillie repeated. "That really surprises me. He was so instrumental in gathering everyone together."

Giovani nodded. "He was having dreams, though; really bad ones. I only knew it because we were rooming together."

Tillie frowned. "I thought you were all having dreams, but they were fading with the black-eye spell gone."

"No." Giovani shook his head. "Not those dreams. I mean, of course he had those too. More like nightmares about his initial kidnapping and about people he hurt while he was an agent, and–"

"Ah." Tillie sipped her tea and set down her hand-thrown ceramic mug with a slight thunk on the table beside her. "You mean trauma dreams."

"I guess so." Giovani fiddled with the handle of his own mug. "Makes you wonder who is next. If someone as strong as Aaron–" He stopped talking and stared down into his tea.

"You're worried you're going to crack next," Tillie observed, leaning forward.

"Of course," said Giovani.

Tillie nodded. "It's certainly possible."

"What?" Giovani's head snapped up. "Aren't you supposed to be comforting me?"

"Supposed to?" Tillie raised her eyebrows. "Aren't we a little off the social convention rails here? I don't think there is any 'supposed to' in this situation. And honestly, I find such conversational practices immensely irritating. No matter who I'm talking to, I'm 'supposed to' tell them that they're the exception to every rule they're concerned about. 'No, no, of course not, not you; you're the strongest and the brightest and the best.'"

Giovani's lips twitched. "Isn't that a big part of your job? Telling your clients how wonderful they are?"

"Sure, but you're not paying me," said Tillie. "So, instead, I'm going to be honest with you. You might crack. Any of us can crack. Hell, I cracked years ago and managed to repair myself. Mostly. But those cracks are still there, just sealed up. A seal can always be broken more easily than a whole piece."

Giovani's eyes met hers. "I'm sorry," he said, softly.

Tillie leaned back in her chair and waved a hand in dismissal. "That's just life. All adults have something, some kind of trauma. Life is rough and complicated and it either cracks you or wears you down or cuts off your legs. We're talking about your trauma right now, though."

She picked up her mug and cradled its warmth in her hands.

"So how do I stop myself from cracking?" said Giovani.

Tillie shrugged. "I have no idea. I've heard that bottling things up is bad. So, I suppose just talking things through like we're doing now is probably step one."

"Sure," said Giovani. "Makes sense. I think physical activity is also supposed to be beneficial, right?"

Tillie paused with her mug halfway up to her lips. Was he propositioning her?

"Plus, I'd like to keep battle-ready," he continued. "So, maybe setting up some sparring time between all of the former agents would be a good way to keep everyone sane and limber."

Apparently not. She brought the tea up to her face and finished her sip, enjoying the warmth of the ginger, the calming effect of the chamomile.

Just as well. Tillie was starting to think maybe her crush on Giovani was something best left behind her. They were working together, after all, and he didn't need to be forming romantic attachments if he was feeling this unsure of himself. It probably wasn't healthy.

"I think that's a fantastic idea," she said, finally. "And it might be nice for them to bring back something familiar. I recall from my brief time with the organization that morning sparring sessions were standard operating procedure, right?"

"Exactly." Giovani sat upright, his voice strengthening now with purpose. "I wonder if the nuns would let us use the school gym in the mornings."

"For now, probably," said Tillie. "But in a couple of months, their school year will start back up again, and they'll probably need it for its intended purpose."

Giovani's body deflated once again. "A couple of months. Honestly, Tillie, I've been living so much just day-to-day. Do you think we'll still be here in a couple of months?"

She looked around. "What do you mean by here, exactly?"

"Not here," he waved his hand to indicate her condo, "I mean, more metaphysically, like here in this event process." He raked a hand through his hair and sighed. "I don't know how to say what I mean. I guess just, how are we taking down the court and the organization? Are we going to stay in St. Louis and use the convent as our base for the long haul? Will it be a long haul? Are we any closer than we were to our eventual goal? Is our eventual goal even possible?"

"Whoa, hey." Tillie lifted her hands and waved at him to stop. "One at a time. These are excellent questions, but let's just slow down."

"How can we slow down when we're not even moving?" Giovani stood and began to pace. "We had one big stand. One huge battle, that we thought was going to decapitate the organization, right? We were going to kill the Pontiff and disable the court, and we thought we had, and now it turns out we didn't do that, and the court seems to be holding their own against us, and all we can do is plan to steal a couple of books?"

Tillie watched him pace and listened to his ranting, but didn't really have anything to add. He was right. It felt pretty hopeless. Then again, they were both natural seers. Planning was what they did. They'd been delving too much into other mage disciplines.

"That's why we keep focusing on the past and the present," she said aloud.

Giovani pivoted on his heel and stared at her. "What?"

She tilted her head back to look into his eyes. "We're not planning. We're seers. Why aren't we planning?"

"Too much morphing." Giovani sank down onto the couch again. "We just can't seem to win. Morphing gets us kidnapped by the Auditors – it's what got us into all this in the first place. It makes us more powerful overall, but it chips away at our strengths, but we have to do it because the court's doing it, and if we don't, we're at a disadvantage."

Tillie shook her head. "You're missing my point. We're still good at planning. We just aren't as *focused* on planning anymore. That's what happens when you morph. You don't lose your strengths; you just lose your focus on those strengths. And I suspect that the court knows that. That's the advantage the court has over us – morphing isn't new to them."

"Nothing is new to them," Giovani pointed out. "They've been around for centuries."

"And that's another mistake we've made," said Tillie.

Giovani cocked his head. "Not being around for centuries?"

"No. Forgetting that they've been around for centuries. How many rebellions exactly like ours do you think they've quelled?"

"Shit. Probably dozens, if not hundreds." Giovani picked up his tea and tossed it back as though taking a shot of whiskey. He grabbed the teapot and poured himself another mug of it.

Tillie watched warily, hoping he wasn't about to shoot down the new tea as well – that pot was well-insulated, and the tea within would be hotter than what was in the mug. She relaxed as he took a careful sip.

"So, we need to be different than those rebellions. Let's take steps to learn about them," she suggested.

"I wouldn't know where to start," said Giovani.

"That's because you're still thinking like a morpher," said Tillie. "We need to return to our strengths. We'll get a stitcher to look into the past. Trevor is fantastic at research. Amy seems like she would be a great choice as well."

Giovani nodded thoughtfully. "You're absolutely right. We do the planning; we base our plans on the research done by stitchers, and we have spellers in charge of executing the plans, because they think well on their feet and can shift those plans when they inevitably go awry."

"Exactly." Tillie nodded vigorously, her bangs falling into her eyes. She pushed them aside. "And then we're on equal footing with the court in one sense at least."

Giovani smiled. "And all the other senses?"

She shrugged. "We'll get there. I believe in us."

6.

Mattie woke up the next morning and bounced up out of bed. She hummed as she bustled about the room, changing into comfy leggings and a tank top and then pulling on her leather armor over that.

She continued humming softly as she strolled down the hallway, smiling at nuns and other guests as she made her way to the convent commissary where the sisters laid out basic breakfast foods each morning.

She grabbed a strawberry yogurt and a glass of orange juice, eating quickly and then hopping back up to head toward the practice room for a little solo workout time before she was supposed to meet up with Sister Margaret for some sparring.

As she worked her way through some burpees and then followed it up with some push-ups – push-ups she wouldn't have been able to do a month ago – she found herself laughing out loud.

She wiped sweat from her brow, standing to start on a round of jumping jacks. "What a fucking hypocrite," she murmured.

"Who?" said Sister Margaret from the doorway.

"Me," said Mattie. She kept jumping, huffing as she spoke. "Just last week, I was making fun of Tillie for starting her day with a work-out and a healthy breakfast."

Sister Margaret frowned. "So, this isn't normal for you?"

Mattie counted out five more jumps and then dropped to the ground for some sit-ups, answering the question in between reps. "I mean, I've never been lazy." Sit-up. "But I always just got my exercise through more . . . " Sit-up. ". . . natural means, like biking and hiking." Sit-up. "It's just more enjoyable for me."

Sister Margaret watched her, chewing on her lip.

Finally, Mattie finished her sit-ups and stood, shaking her limbs out. "Something bugging you?"

"Just something your sister said."

"What's that?" said Mattie.

"Would you say that you've changed your lifestyle completely?" said Sister Margaret. "You've really been throwing yourself into studying magery and learning to fight."

Mattie cocked her head. "Yeah, so? I'm not sure what you're getting at."

Sister Margaret shook her head. "Fuck it. I'm no good at being subtle. Tillie and Trevor are worried you're getting too hyperfocused and you'll burn yourself out. Apparently, you've done this before."

Mattie narrowed her eyes and crossed her arms, a scowl forming on her face. "Those busybody little–"

"No." Sister Margaret cut her off. "They're not busybodies. They're your family and they want to make sure you're taking care of yourself."

"Potato, potahto."

"It's not a potahto!" Sister Margaret leaned against the wall and crossed her own arms, mirroring Mattie's stance. "Also, nobody says 'potahto.' I've never heard a single person ever pronounce it that way!"

"I think maybe British people do," Mattie suggested. "Anyway, Tillie doesn't know what she's talking about. You said that I don't know her, well, she doesn't know me any better. I've changed since college."

"What about Trevor?" said Sister Margaret. "Does he know you?"

Mattie pursed her lips as she considered the point. "Look," she said, finally. She plopped herself down on a bench against the mirrored wall. "They're right that I've done that in the past. Maybe they're not wrong to be concerned. But they're wrong about what's happening now. I'm not hyperfocused. Or, if I am, it's because honestly, I feel alive for the first time in years. Maybe ever. I don't know if I've ever really felt alive."

Sister Margaret's eyes widened and she exhaled with a whoosh. "That is some heavy shit, amiga. You gotta do what you gotta do to feel alive."

"Yeah." Mattie closed her eyes and then popped them open again. "Shall we spar?"

"It's open," called Tillie in response to a knock on her condo door. Must be Amy – Trevor would know to just come on in.

She sipped her smoothie and smiled. It felt like it was becoming more and more rare that she was able to get a proper amount of sleep and start her day off right with a work-out, a smoothie, and good company.

The door opened a little and Amy poked her head around it. "Hello?" she called.

Tillie picked up her glass and strode into the living room. "Hello! Have you eaten? I think Trevor is bringing some kind of pastry assortment, but I could make you a smoothie in the meantime."

"Oh, thank you," said Amy. "I'm good for now."

"Tea?" said Tillie. "I think I might even have some coffee around here somewhere."

Amy hesitated. "If it's not too much trouble."

Tillie waved a dismissive hand. "Not at all!" She paused. "Was that for tea or for coffee?"

"I don't want to make you hunt it down," said Amy with a smile. "Tea sounds great."

"Earl Grey?"

"Perfect."

Tillie ambled back into the kitchen, and Amy followed. "Giovani's still asleep in the guest room. I figured it's best that he gets his rest and joins us whenever he's ready."

"We'll need everyone at full performance level if we're going to pull this off," Amy agreed. "I've been thinking a lot about how we're going to do it."

"It seems very daunting, to be honest," said Tillie, switching on the electric kettle with a click. "You're the only one who has seen the books, so you'll have to be the only one actually doing the stitching."

"And the range is a lot farther than should really be possible," said Amy. "Plus, it's been a couple of years since I've been into the base, so things might have moved around. And to top it all off, who knows what kind of protective magics they have protecting the base?"

Tillie nodded thoughtfully, leaning on the counter with her arms outstretched. "Step one should be to scry in. See if we can even see the books at this range and through any shields they'll have up."

"And hope that it doesn't trip some kind of alarm," Amy added. "That was my thought as well. Being a seer, I assume you have high quality scrying equipment."

Tillie nodded again, although it hadn't been framed as a question. "I've also done quite a lot of group magics in the past, so my ritual room is set up to amplify such things."

Amy's eyebrows rose. "Ritual room?"

Tillie waved in the general direction of the secret room. "All the condos in this building come equipped with a secret room for magery. Few of us who live here came from mage families, so it's really nice to be able to keep it . . . out of the way."

"That sounds very fancy." Amy looked around the kitchen with interest. "I never lived in a place like this, with a whole mage community. Aside from the Auditor stations, of course, but that's not exactly the same."

"It's nice to have a community," Tillie agreed with a smile.

She heard the front door open. Trevor must have arrived. "In here," she called.

Trevor strode into room, a large plastic-covered tray in his hands. "I stopped by work to pick up my last check," he said. "These are day-olds, but still always tasty."

He worked for a large chain of warehouse stores and had elected to take a few weeks' medical leave, implying to his bosses that he had some kind of serious illness that needed intense treatment, and leaving the rest to their imagination.

Tillie hoped he'd be able to return to his job soon, but she was grateful he was willing to take the time off – he'd worked at that job ever since finishing grad school and realizing that the job market for Medieval history specialists wasn't as thriving as he'd hoped.

Trevor set down the platter of pastries and peeled off its filmy covering, selecting a large bear claw for himself.

Amy daintily poked around a little and then took something sprinkled with poppy seeds.

As Tillie snagged herself a chocolate croissant, Giovani finally wandered into the kitchen, dressed in flannel pants and a black t-shirt, rubbing his eyes groggily.

"Morning, sunshine," she said cheerfully.

"Everyone's here, huh?" Giovani yawned hugely and plopped onto a bar stool, reaching for the pastries and pulling the entire tray toward himself. "Is there coffee?"

The kettle clicked off and Tillie moved to pour the water over the leaves she had already placed in her largest teapot. "Tea will be ready in a few minutes."

Giovani muttered something under his breath.

"What was that?" Tillie asked sharply.

He glanced up at her and shrank back a little. "Tea sounds great," he replied.

"Uh huh."

Mattie toweled off her hair as she walked from the communal shower room down the hall to her bedroom.

She glanced at the glowing numbers on the nightstand alarm clock: ten minutes after ten. She had almost an hour to kill before she was due for a stitching lesson from Sister Catherine, and then back to training with Sister Margaret at eleven-thirty.

Tossing her towel on the back of a wooden chair, she ran a brush through her long, still-damp hair and then tugged it into a loose braid.

She looked around the room, at a loss for how to fill the time. Her eyes landed on a book Sister Margaret had lent her on scrying. Since that would be the subject of their training today, she might as well get a jump on the material.

Mattie grabbed the book and sat down on the bed, back against the wall, legs stretched out in front of her. She began to read.

Tillie pulled the key to the ritual room out of her desk drawer. To the untrained eye, the key looked like a pendant with the mage sign for seers on it: an hourglass for magery, topped with a stylized eye to show the particular discipline.

She had the same symbol tattooed on her hip. As she fitted the symbol into the matching divot on the linen closet door, she idly wondered if maybe she should consider adding the other symbols to the tattoo, making it a morphing symbol.

After all, Tillie was no longer merely a seer. Someone should design a new symbol; it could be a rallying point for their movement.

She stepped back and waited as the spell activated and the door slid sideways. Once it stopped moving, she opened the door and stepped inside, flipping on the light as she did so, and then dimming it a little bit for the sake of her scrying projection spell.

Tillie hurried to the front of the room, arranging everything on her altar into an optimal configuration for group scrying.

She pulled down the white retractable screen that hung from the ceiling, then bustled around to stand in front of the altar. "Okay, so I have this set up with a spell that will automatically project anything scried into this crystal onto that screen." She indicated the crystal that was built into the center of the table, moving aside her smaller, portable stones. "You can all go ahead and take seats – the room is set up with more spells so that any occupied couches will be connected together to easily share mage energy without touching."

Amy whistled softly. "This is really fascinating. How did you set all this up? I've never seen anything like it; not even in an Auditor station. Not even in the court's rooms."

Tillie shrugged. "It's a very forward-thinking building. People work together a lot, both to set up the rooms and using them for complex magics."

She felt a little bit sad as she thought about how much fun she'd had in the past with friends and neighbors, just playing around with what kinds of magics they could all do together.

Stephanie always wanted to combine magic and tech, which had been particularly interesting.

"Is there a configuration that will be most beneficial for us to sit in?" asked Trevor, interrupting her train of thought.

"Not really," said Tillie. "We've done lots of experiments with different seating arrangements, and it all pretty much boils down to how many people and what disciplines are present, rather than where everyone is sitting."

Trevor nodded and chose a seat on the couch closest to Tillie's altar. Amy sat down beside him on the same couch, while Giovani went for the one directly behind them.

"Okay, so we'll start by scrying out this bunker in Utah," said Tillie. "I was thinking I would do the scrying, but Amy, if you're able to, it might be easier for you, since you've been there before."

Amy looked startled. "I – I haven't scried since before – before I was taken by the Auditors," she stammered.

"But you have done it before," Tillie observed.

"Well, yes." Amy chewed on her bottom lip. She visibly steeled herself, exhaling audibly and straightening her spine. She lifted her head and met Tillie's eyes. "I'll do my best."

Trevor took her hand and squeezed it, giving her a warm, encouraging smile. "We'll be right here, lending you our strength."

Amy nodded and stood to join Tillie at the altar. Tillie turned to face the stone and the screen behind it. "Do you remember how to move your eyes into seer mode?"

"I think so," said Amy.

Tillie noted the tension gathering in Amy's neck and shoulders. "Try and relax. Shake yourself out a little bit." She demonstrated, loosening her limbs and moving her torso back and forth so her arms shook by her sides.

Amy followed suit.

"Now, I know this seems counterintuitive, but I think it helps to close your eyes first," Tillie instructed.

Amy closed her eyes, placing her hands on the stone of the altar. That was good – by touching the altar, she would be able to tap into the energies of the people sitting on the couches.

Tillie placed a hand on Amy's back to lend her own energies as well. "Breathe in deeply." She waited for Amy to do so and then continued. "Now think about how much you want to see clearly. You want to see into the future and you want to see what's happening far away, and you want it so badly that you might just burst."

Amy's eyes flew open and they were pure white. "That was easy!" she exclaimed. "I don't think it was that easy before."

"Well," said Tillie. "You're connected to all of us. Do you think you can scry out this bunker?"

"I actually think I can," said Amy, her voice filled with wonder. "Let's do this!"

Trevor applauded and Giovani joined in.

Tillie contented herself with a broad grin, keeping her hand in contact with the seeing stitcher so as to not deprive her of any mage power.

This was a long way to see, and Amy was rusty – she was going to need all the help she could get.

"Peer into the scrying stone," said Tillie. "And picture the room you want to see. The room with the books."

Amy leaned forward, both hands on the table and placed her face almost right up against the smooth round clear quartz. For several minutes, nothing happened.

Tillie continued to pour mage energy into Amy, waiting patiently. It was difficult to scry long distances even for a natural seer like herself, and Amy was on the other end of the mage spectrum.

Finally, a picture began to form slowly on the screen behind the altar, blurry at first and then gradually swimming into focus.

The screen showed a small, cozy room, floor-to-ceiling bookcases lining all the walls, with a seating area in the middle – two brown easy chairs and a matching loveseat. Beside each seat was a well-worn wooden end table, and a coffee table in the middle pulled the room together.

Each seat also had a standing lamp behind it for optimal reading light.

The bookcases were stuffed full of scholarly-looking tomes and a rolling ladder granted access to the upper shelves.

"Oooooooh," said Trevor. "That looks like my perfect vacation spot."

"If only it wasn't in an underground bunker full of assholes," agreed Giovani.

"I don't mind the underground bunker part," said Trevor. "But I could do without the assholes."

"If we could focus, please," said Tillie. "Amy? Any particular books you remember that you want to grab?"

"I don't think I can stitch and hold the picture at the same time," said Amy, through gritted teeth.

Tillie poured more energy into her.

"If you can direct me to the right books, I'll try and stitch them out," Trevor offered. "I have never stitched anything this far, but at least books are smaller than people, and I've stitched a lot of those."

"Nobody could stitch a person, not even just themself, that far," said Tillie. "Even with us boosting you."

"But a book?" said Giovani. "I bet you can."

"Let's find out," said Amy. The picture zoomed in on a bookshelf and began to slowly travel upward. After scanning a couple of shelves, she stopped and zoomed in further, one title filling the screen.

Secrets of the Ancient Court, the spine read.

"That sounds promising," said Giovani.

Tillie's back was to Trevor, so she didn't see him stitch, but the book suddenly disappeared from the picture.

She twisted her head around, careful to keep her hands on Amy's back, and saw Trevor triumphantly holding it up.

"I got it!" His voice sounded a little bit winded. "I think I have at least one more stitch in me."

Tillie was also feeling tired – between Amy's scrying and Trevor's stitching, the group as a whole was using up a lot of mage power to reach something so far away.

As Tillie turned back toward the picture on the screen, Amy scanned the shelves again, eventually landing on another book: *Gone Rogue: A History of Agent Uprisings.*

A moment later, it too sat beside Trevor on his black couch.

Tillie could feel Amy starting to tremble and she was sure Trevor was in a similar state. "Let's take a break," she suggested.

Amy immediately sagged, leaning fully against the altar, and the projected picture disappeared.

Tillie checked the time on the step tracker strapped to her wrist. "Wow! We've been in here for over two hours. Let's have some lunch."

Mattie sagged in her chair, leaning back from the small table with the stone set in the center. "I don't know why, but seeing is a lot harder for me than stitching," she commented.

"You'd think it would be the same," said Sister Margaret. "Since spelling is right in the middle of those, right?"

Mattie shrugged. "You tell me. I'm still learning all of this."

Sister Margaret stood. "Well, I've never actually trained anyone to see who wasn't a natural seer. Hell, I've only really trained a couple of people to see at all. And mostly then I was just teaching them to use their seer abilities while fighting."

Mattie stood as well. "I appreciate you teaching me."

"It's all good." Sister Margaret waved her thanks away. "Never hurts for me to practice teaching."

"Lunch?" said Mattie, jerking her head toward the commissary.

"For sure." Sister Margaret led the way out of the room.

"Do you want to be teaching more?" asked Mattie as they walked.

"Not really," Sister Margaret admitted. "At least not here in the school. I don't have the patience."

"So, how come you're here, then? I mean, if you're not interested in teaching kids, why belong to an order of teachers?"

"We're not an order of teachers," Sister Margaret corrected. "We're an order of warriors. Some of those warriors are teachers, yes, and even some of the sisters whose designation isn't Teacher do teach. But this is just one convent of our order among hundreds, and most of them aren't schools."

"What are the others?" Mattie stepped up beside the nun at the buffet line, and surveyed the options, which mostly consisted of a variety of sandwich and wrap platters. She snagged half of a wrap that looked like it had chicken, bacon, some green veggies, and some kind of white dressing, and then loaded up the rest of her plate with blue tortilla chips and a glob of guacamole.

Sister Margaret loaded up a plate of her own and led the way to an out-of-the-way table before responding. "Lots of things. We run schools, yes, but also nursing homes, safe houses, group homes for foster kids, a couple of hospitals, and archives."

"Archives?" said Mattie. "Like libraries?"

Sister Margaret nodded enthusiastically. "Incredible libraries. You've never seen libraries like these."

"Really?" Mattie leaned forward. "What do you mean?"

"Well, I've never seen them either," said Sister Margaret. "But I want to. I really, really want to. They're supposed to be just absolutely wild and magical – filled with books people would kill to get their hands on. And have."

"Books on magery?" asked Mattie

"Magery, history, science, the truth about the world. All kinds of things," said Sister Margaret. She took a big bite of her sandwich, and Mattie waited for her to finish chewing. "And all of them are super secret. In out-of-the-way, dangerous places, staffed by only the best Warrior Mage Librarians."

Mattie smiled at the excitement in Sister Margaret's voice. "I'm guessing you have ambitions in that direction."

"Fuck, yeah," said Sister Margaret. "I absolutely want to be a WML. Life fucking goals, right there."

"It does sound kind of awesome," Mattie admitted. "I don't think I could do it, though."

"Why not?" Sister Margaret frowned.

"Don't you have to be a nun?"

Sister Margaret waved a hand and shook her head vigorously. "No, no. I'd say about half of the WMLs out there are lay people. You don't even really have to be Catholic. The Vatican gets less picky about the more niche kinds of jobs like that. They probably wouldn't be able to find enough people to do them if they had strict rules. You just have to be a badass who likes books, really."

"Hmmm." Mattie thought it over as she ate her wrap.

"Damn, I love books," said Trevor. He held one of their new acquisitions up to his face and inhaled deeply.

"Even evil books?" said Amy with a teasing waggle of her eyebrows.

"Especially evil books!" said Trevor with relish.

"Especially? Really?" Giovani cocked his head. "I would honestly much prefer to steer clear of evil things in general."

Tillie nodded emphatically. "I mean, don't get me wrong; I'm glad we have them, but if I had my druthers, we'd be sticking to non-evil reading material. I'll be happy when all of this is over."

"If it's ever over," said Trevor, cheerfully. He led the way into the kitchen and opened the fridge, poking his head inside.

Tillie shivered. "Don't talk like that. It has to end sometime, right?"

"I don't know," said Amy, thoughtfully. "I mean, I guess it can be over for any of us at any time, either by dying in battle or by just giving up and leaving. Enough people have done both. And no one would blame you for leaving."

Tillie blinked. Oddly enough, even though she had sympathized with the people who had washed their hands of the whole fight, it somehow had never occurred to her that she could do the same. She felt so responsible for the whole thing, but when it came right down to it, she had been a victim of the Auditor organization.

It was just a coincidence that she happened to have been targeted at the same time Giovani was deserting and that the agent sent after her was the rebellious Agent Miller and that the court came to St. Louis at that particular time.

That was a lot of coincidences. Maybe there was some kind of fate involved.

Tillie hated the idea of fate. Her cat jumped up onto the stool in front of her, and she absently scratched his ears. It might be a good idea to see if she could take Max back over to her neighbor's condo to stay for a while; she was spending an awful lot of time away, and it wasn't fair to the poor kitty, who was used to getting lots of love from her.

Trevor had moved onto the freezer drawer, and pulled out a veggie lasagna. "How does this sound to everyone?"

"Do it in the microwave or it takes about 90 minutes," said Tillie.

"Will do," said Trevor, giving her a finger-gun salute. As he bustled around her kitchen, prepping the lasagna and starting the microwave, pouring glasses of water, and putting some veggie chips into a bowl, Tillie pulled one of the books toward her and opened it up.

Honestly, she would never be able to live with herself if she abandoned her friends; the best way to get out of the whole situation was going to be to win.

7.

Mattie finished lunch and parted ways with Sister Margaret. At loose ends once again, she wandered back to her bedroom.

She eyed her armor, which was hanging in the closet, visible through the open door. Maybe she should see if anyone was around and looking for a sparring partner.

Pulling her phone out of the back pocket of her jeans, Mattie shot off a quick text message to Nicole.

The phone chirped back immediately. Nicole was just finishing up a meeting with a few other former Auditors – the ones who had come back to get their black-eye spell lifted – and would meet her at the sparring studios in twenty minutes.

With a grin, Mattie changed into leggings and donned the armor over the top.

She took off down the hall again at a brisk walk.

Before she got to the stairs that would take her down to the common areas, Cardinal Neubacher emerged from a bedroom. "Ah, Ms. Holiday," he said in that smooth way of his, as he fell into step beside her.

Mattie remembered what Sister Catherine had said about staying on his good side and gave him a bland smile. "Call me Mattie, please," she said.

"Certainly. Mattie. How is your training going?"

"Very well, I hope," she said. "I'm learning a lot from Sister Catherine and Sister Margaret. Magery and fighting."

"Glad to hear it," he said. "The world can always use more warriors in the fight against evil."

"Like Ida," she said, softly. "Your eulogy was very moving, Father. And very motivating."

Cardinal Neubacher's eyebrows rose. "Tell me, Mattie. Are you a Catholic, yourself?"

"Uh, no," she said. "I'm not. I wasn't really raised anything religious at all."

"Ah," he said. "Then perhaps you can be forgiven for not using the proper address for a Cardinal such as myself."

Mattie narrowed her eyes. The proper address? This pompous asshole was going to lecture her about a proper address? But she didn't want to cause trouble for Sister Catherine, so she simply said, stiffly, "I'm sorry. What would the proper address have been?"

He paused in his step, forcing her to stop walking as well, as he studied her. "'Your Eminence' is traditional, but 'Cardinal' is also acceptable. 'Father' refers to a priest. A bishop would be addressed as 'Your Excellency.'"

Mattie's eyes widened as she tried to hold in the laughter that was trying to bubble to the surface. These titles weren't quite as ridiculous as those used by the Auditors, but seriously, how pretentious could you get? She managed to barely quell her amusement as she replied, "My apologies. Your Eminence."

Cardinal Neubacher smiled and continued walking. "No apology necessary. I merely wanted you to know for future reference. Not everyone in the higher echelons of the Church is as forgiving or as informal as I am."

Mattie gratefully lunged for the door to the stairwell. "Okay, well, thanks," she babbled. "This is me. Catch you later, Your Eminence." She shut the door behind her and peered through the plexiglass window, watching as he proceeded down the hall.

When she had judged him far enough away that he wouldn't hear, Mattie finally let loose a long, hearty peal of laughter.

As they ate their lasagna, Tillie, Trevor, Amy, and Giovani took turns reading aloud from the first book they'd grabbed, *Secrets of the Ancient Court.*

It was a fascinating history of how the organization started and the first few centuries in which it went from being a known and open society among many others of its kind, to the decision to fake its own dissolution and go underground.

Unfortunately, however, it didn't actually contain any secret magics, which was what they'd been hoping to find.

Tillie gathered up the plates and stacked them in the sink; she would get to them later. "Shall we crack open the other book or try and stitch more out?" she asked.

"I vote to pull more books," said Amy. "I'm concerned that if they notice these are missing, they could set up shields or even traps. It's best to grab as many books as we can first, and then start reading them."

"That makes sense," said Giovani. "And I believe that I can take over as seer, having been a part of the group work this morning."

"That would be perfect," said Amy. "Then we'll have two stitchers on the job and can grab twice as many books." She smacked her hand down on the countertop for emphasis. "We have *got* to find something that will tell us what the hell kind of spells they have over us or we're just sitting ducks next time they decide to activate something."

"Agreed," said Giovani. "I can scry for longer, being a natural seer."

"If the two of us split the work, we can get even more mileage," said Tillie. She gestured toward the ritual room. "Let's get back to work."

Mattie raised her practice blade just in time to block Nicole's thrust, and then twisted it, trying to disarm her opponent. Nicole deftly pulled her weapon free and returned with a smooth spin, her momentum carrying her into a heavy blow to Mattie's shoulder.

Dancing back, Mattie winced a little, minutely wiggling her arm to test out the extent of the damage. Determining that it would result in nothing more than a bruise, she quickly darted forward, catching Nicole off guard and forcing her backward toward the mirrored wall.

Nicole turned the tables once more, and Mattie danced back again. "How did the meeting go?" she asked, as they circled each other, looking for openings.

"Good, actually," said Nicole. "I didn't have high hopes, but they've all decided to stick around, at least for a while."

"Oh, nice," said Mattie. "What changed their minds?"

"Well," said Nicole. She lunged forward, forcing Mattie back. "They weren't doing great on their own, as it turns out."

Mattie saw an opening and stabbed her sword forward toward Nicole's belly.

Nicole swept her own sword down, blocking the move.

"It must be hard to adjust to living an ordinary life," said Mattie. She pushed forward with a flurry of slashes, all of which Nicole blocked. "Even with the resources we gave them."

Nicole nodded and attacked. Mattie ducked and spun, evading the sword by barely an inch.

"So, they figured it might be better to stay and fight," said Nicole. "Pause."

Mattie stopped attacking and stepped back. She walked over to the bench and grabbed two white towels from a stack that sat at one end, tossing one to Nicole and wiping her brow with the other.

Nicole caught it deftly, wiping off her own face and taking a long pull from a water bottle.

"Are they going to stay here in the convent?" Mattie asked.

Nicole shook her head. "Donna's going to move into your old room with me and Denise. The guys will move into Aaron and Giovani's place."

Mattie raised her eyebrows. "Where will Aaron and Giovani go?"

"Aaron left." Nicole took another drink of water. "And Giovani has been crashing at your sister's, so he said his room was up for grabs."

Mattie laughed. "Has he now?"

"I don't think it's like that, actually," said Nicole.

"Not yet," said Mattie. "But I know Tillie."

Nicole frowned. "I mean, I know she used to be. . ." she trailed off before continuing, " . . . but isn't she retired?"

Mattie's eyebrows raised. "I'm not suggesting that Tillie's got Giovani as some kind of live-in john. I just mean that Giovani's absolutely her type. Like for an actual relationship. And she's been making eyes at him literally since they met."

Nicole blushed. "I'm sorry. I didn't mean to jump to conclusions. I've never known any . . ."

"Sex workers," Mattie supplied. "The term is 'sex workers.' Believe me – if you try to use any other term, Tillie will bite your head off, but in a very sweet and polite sort of way that somehow makes you feel much worse than if she was yelling."

Nicole grinned. "That sounds like Tillie." She set down her water bottle. "Okay, I'm ready if you are."

Mattie dropped her towel and lifted her sword again in a ready position.

Fed and refreshed, they managed to work for six hours, getting book after book after book. Tillie and Giovani took turns taking lead on the scrying, while Amy and Trevor did the same with the stitching.

By the time Trevor finally called a halt to it, the day had turned to evening and there was a stack of fifteen books sitting on the couch between Amy and Trevor.

"I'm sorry," said Trevor. His voice broke slightly in his exhaustion. "I just don't think I can keep going."

Tillie blinked her eyes, moving out of seer mode, and the picture on the screen disappeared abruptly. "I'm just about at the end of my reserves too," she admitted. She probably could have kept going for about half an hour, but one or two more books weren't worth running herself – and the others – ragged.

She stumbled to the couch directly behind the stitchers and collapsed. Giovani plopped down beside her. "We did good," he said, running his hands through his hair.

"We really did, didn't we?" said Amy, holding up one of the books with a triumphant flourish. She seemed to have the most energy left out of any of them.

Tillie squinted at the title on the book Amy was still brandishing. *Quelling the Masses: Standardizing Sleeper Spells.*

"That one has to have some helpful stuff in it," she observed. "The spells themselves, if not how to break them."

"I bet you dollars to donuts it's got the black-eye spell," Amy agreed.

"I don't think I'm up for breaking into anything tonight, though," said Giovani. "Should we meet back here first thing tomorrow for study time?"

"We should probably take them to the convent, don't you think?" Trevor objected.

"I'm staying there," said Amy. "I'll stitch them into my bedroom, and then we can meet tomorrow and see if anyone wants to help us come through them."

"Sounds good to me," said Tillie. Early as it was, all she wanted to do at that moment was go to sleep. She glanced at her wrist. It was 7:30. She didn't even care.

Amy moved her fingers and they glowed as the books disappeared.

"I need to head home," said Trevor. "I'm going to sleep like the dead tonight."

"Same," said Amy.

The stitchers left, and with barely another word, Tillie and Giovani each went into their own rooms and crashed.

8.

Mattie woke up very suddenly at the sound of shouting and threw off the covers, revealing bare legs and a thin gray tank top. She stumbled a little as she rushed toward the door of the narrow bedroom she was currently occupying in the convent.

The commotion was still on-going outside in the hallway, and as she flung open her door, nuns and other guests alike were rushing past, some still boiling out of their bedrooms, some already on their way away from the dorm wing and toward the common areas.

A familiar form rushed by, and Mattie snagged Sister Regina's arm, stopping her. "What's going on?" she demanded.

The nun was dressed in fuzzy pajamas with pictures of cats on them. Her head, usually adorned with a perpetually crooked whimple, was bare, showing her blonde hair, flat on one side and frizzy on the other. She pulled her arm free. "Something about Agent Shezza. Sister Margaret's waiting for everyone in the meeting hall."

The nun resumed her headlong dash down the corridor and Mattie paused to grab a pair of jeans off the floor, and then pelted after Sister Regina without bothering to pull them on over her purple briefs.

She reached the door to the meeting hall and noticed the scandalized look of an elderly nun she had only met once or twice. Sister Ann or Elaine or something like that.

Mattie paused and stepped out of the stream of people to put her pants on, and then entered the room, glancing around.

She didn't see Sister Margaret anywhere, but Sister Catherine and Cardinal Neubacher were standing at the front of the room, talking in hushed voices, so she strode toward them, ignoring the rows of seats that were quickly filling up.

"You!" Cardinal Neubacher hissed at her as she marched up to him. "If you hadn't butted your nose in where it didn't belong yesterday, Shezza and I would be on a private jet somewhere over the Atlantic Ocean right now. Instead, she's managed to break out of her cell and is loose somewhere in the building, assuming she hasn't broken out completely and gotten halfway to an Auditor safe house!"

Mattie's eyes narrowed. "You're blaming me because you lost control of your prisoner? So much for the hot shot from the Vatican."

Sister Catherine stepped between them. "Blame has never gotten anyone where they needed to go. We're not even sure what exactly happened." She turned to Cardinal Neubacher. "I'll thank you to remember where you are, Cardinal. She will not have escaped this building."

Mattie smirked.

Sister Catherine raised an eyebrow at her. "And as for you, young lady, what did I tell you about giving respect where it's due?"

Mattie's grin turned into a scowl, but she muttered an apology.

Cardinal Neubacher nodded a regal acceptance.

Just then, Sister Margaret strode into the room, immaculately clad in her leather armor and armed to the teeth, her black hair pulled back into a long, tidy braid, even at this time of the night.

Mattie glanced at the clock as she took a seat in the front row – three o'clock in the morning. Did Sister Margaret ever sleep?

Sister Margaret lifted her arms and the nervous chatter died down. "Thank you all for gathering here at this hour. I will cut straight to the chase. Our lockdown system has been activated for the second time in as many weeks. This may sound dire to some, but in reality, our order was formed for this, trained for it. We are warrior mages. That said, this facility is primarily a school and a prison, and I know that many of you here signed on to be teachers or guards, and are warriors secondarily.

"This situation may feel less dangerous than the last – after all, it is only one missing person, and not an entire wing of suddenly empty cells. But this woman, this so-called Agent Shezza – we know that isn't her real name, but we don't know what her name is – should be treated as extremely cunning, volatile, and powerful. I suspect that what we have seen from her is only a small fraction of what she is capable of.

"And she might be desperate." Sister Margaret let out a small, bitter chuckle. "On the one hand, I kind of hope she is, because that would mean that we are actually making a dent in her psyche. But on the other hand, desperate people are willing to do things that others aren't, so desperation makes her that much more dangerous."

She paused and looked around the room. "We need to catch her as soon as we can and get her into one of the high security cells. I know we had her in an observation cell, and that seemed advantageous at the time, but we won't make the mistake of underestimating Shezza again.

"And to the point of not underestimating her, I don't want just anyone going after her. Most of you will be ill-equipped to handle her."

Mattie straightened her back. Would she be deemed skilled enough to go after the spy? She hoped so. She had no intention of sitting this one out.

Sister Margaret continued. "I want Sisters Catherine, Regina, and Helen on the case, along with Mattie and any of the former Auditor agents who are here and feeling up for it. The rest of you may be dismissed."

As most of the sisters shuffled out of the room, along with a few of the former agents – apparently they weren't feeling up for it – Mattie allowed herself a small, triumphant smile. All of her hard work and training was paying off.

She paused as she watched one sister who hadn't been asked to stay behind making her way up to the front of the room. Sister Timothy Ann seemed like a nice woman, but definitely not very fierce, and she was presumably one of those who wouldn't be able to hold her own against Shezza.

Curious, Mattie followed Sister Tim over to where she was conferring with Sister Margaret and Cardinal Neubacher.

"–talented WMS, specializing in chemistry," Sister Margaret was saying as she introduced Sister Tim to the Cardinal.

Mattie wondered what a WMS was, but kept quiet, listening for clues rather than demanding answers.

"Ah, yes," said Cardinal Neubacher, his eyes sharpening in interest. "I thought I recognized your name. You're one of the ones working on that truth spell, are you not?"

Sister Timothy Ann nodded enthusiastically. "That's exactly what I wanted to talk to you about. I believe I may have cracked it!"

"That will be invaluable once we find the fugitive," said Cardinal Neubacher. "I would very much like to see a demonstration if you have time right now."

"Absolutely," said Sister Tim. "My lab is this way." She jerked her head toward the door and began to walk away, the Cardinal hot on her heels.

"What's a WMS?" Mattie asked Sister Margaret.

"Warrior Mage Scientist," said Sister Margaret absently. "Have a seat; we need to break into teams and get moving."

That didn't really answer her question at all, and in fact brought up several more questions, but Mattie recognized that this wasn't the time.

She took a seat and waited for her instructions.

Tillie sat up in bed and glanced at the clock on her nightstand. Four o'clock in the morning. She lay back down and closed her eyes, but her mind was wide awake.

"Might as well get up," she muttered a few minutes later. She swung her legs over the side of her king-sized bed, tossing the satin sheets and organic cotton comforter off to the side.

Tillie stepped into the slippers she'd left on the floor just where she knew her feet would land, stood up, and stretched luxuriantly. She rolled her neck back and forth a couple of times, working out the kinks, and then strode to her dresser, where she'd left a set of morning work-out clothes.

After changing out of her nightgown, Tillie ambled over to the corner where her yoga mat lived, shuffled back out of her slippers, and began her routine, starting with krav maga exercises and then transitioning into yoga, moving instinctively through the poses, letting her body decide what it needed most.

Tillie finished seated with her legs crossed and her hands palm-up on her knees, breathing deeply with her eyes closed.

A sudden crashing sound from her living room had her leaping to her feet, her eyes snapping open and into seer mode as she whirled around and pelted out of her bedroom, nearly wrenching her arm out of its socket as she flung open the door.

She emerged from the hallway into the living room and stared at a sheepish Giovani, who stood over a broken mug on the floor, its shards surrounded by steaming liquid.

"Sorry," he said. "I was trying really hard to be quiet."

Tillie switched her eyes back to normal with a sigh of relief. "Don't worry about it. I was already up anyway." She hurried into the kitchen to grab a towel.

When she returned, Giovani had picked up the ceramic pieces and was standing uncertainly with them in his hands.

Tillie held out both hands, offering the towel with one and leaving the other empty for him to give her the broken mug. Fortunately, it wasn't one of her beautiful, one-of-a-kind artisan mugs – just a cheesy one that she didn't recognize. It depicted a now-split-in-half cartoon dog and the words *It's a Dog's Life*. Mattie must have left it behind.

Once Giovani took the towel from her, she carefully cradled the shards in both hands, taking care not to cut herself on a sharp edge as she walked slowly back into the kitchen, standing on one foot to wave the other near the motion sensor that opened the sleek chrome garbage can.

Then she walked back into the living room to relieve Giovani of the now sopping wet and warm towel. She disposed of the rag in the laundry hamper in the bathroom and returned to the kitchen to make the two of them a new batch of tea.

"I'm sorry about the mug," said Giovani, taking a seat on one of the bar stools at the kitchen island.

Tillie shrugged. "I think that one must have been Mattie's; it's not mine."

"I did try to use one that didn't seem much like you," he admitted. "Not because I thought I'd be breaking it, but just in case you had one that you would want to drink out of whenever you got up."

Tillie turned on the kettle and gave him a warm smile. "That was considerate. Thank you. What are you doing up so early?"

"I'm not sure. I woke up about–" he glanced at the clock over the stove. "Ninety minutes ago, and couldn't get back to sleep. Just had a bad feeling."

Tillie nodded. "Me too. Well, half an hour ago. But I had a bad feeling too."

"I texted a couple of people to see if anything was happening at the convent," said Giovani. "I haven't heard back, but I wouldn't expect to at this time of night."

"Unless something actually was happening," said Tillie. "But then again, if something is happening, they might be too busy to respond to a text."

Giovani nodded, thoughtfully. "It can't be a coincidence that two strong seers both have a bad feeling and can't sleep."

Tillie lifted an eyebrow. "Wouldn't you think at least one of us would have had some kind of vision? I've never had just a 'bad feeling' without an actual vision of what caused it before."

"Maybe it's another sign of the weakening of our seer nature," Giovani suggested. "Maybe this is how natural seers who aren't trained feel."

Tillie nodded. "Now that you mention it, I used to feel like this sometimes before I became a mage. So I guess I shouldn't say 'never.'"

Giovani blinked. "Sometimes I forget that there are mages who weren't just . . . always mages. I was born into a mage family. I don't even remember a time when I wasn't a seer. I must have started training as a toddler, alongside walking and talking."

"It wouldn't be so bad with a seer, but I would hate to be the parent of a spelling or stitching toddler," Tillie laughed. "Not that I ever want to be a mother at all. But that sounds particularly nightmarish."

"You don't?" Giovani cocked his head. "Not ever?"

Tillie suddenly remembered that Giovani had a son of his own. Where was the kid? Most of the former agents who had offspring among the court had gone back to their families, taking the children with them. Many of them had taken extra children, since most of the liberated youth needed a place to go.

"I wish I could be a better father," Giovani continued, a note of wistfulness entering his voice. "I've tried to be as much a part of Marco's life as much as I could, but the way the organization raises their progeny is complicated. And I felt like I would be doing him a disservice if I took him in while I'm working on taking them down now."

"So, where is he now?" Tillie asked.

"My dad took him in," said Giovani. "I'm sure he's being completely and utterly spoiled, but he's a good kid – he'll come through it without turning into a brat. And after what he's been through, it might even do him some good to feel loved for himself and not just because he's a talented mage."

Tillie remembered Giovani's father from the battle at Auditor HQ; a stern and dignified man with the signature Garaveldi heavy eyebrows. She tried to imagine him as a doting grandfather, but came up empty.

The electric kettle beeped and shut itself off, and Tillie poured the hot water over the tea leaves she'd already measured out into her teapot's diffuser. As soon as the water hit the leaves, the scent of bergamot and black tea wafted upward.

"Maybe we should scry out the convent," she suggested. "Just to make sure nothing terrible is happening."

Without waiting for Giovani to respond, she moved her fingers in a stitch, bringing her scrying stone into the kitchen from its home on the altar in her ritual room. The large crystal appeared on the counter beside her and she turned to place it on the island between herself and Giovani.

Giovani leaned forward to peer into the stone, his eyes turning white as he did so.

Tillie turned back around, and strode to the fridge to grab some fruit for her breakfast.

"What the hell?" said Giovani behind her.

She spun around. "What do you see?"

"Nothing," said Giovani, lifting his gaze from the stone. "All I can see is the outside of the convent. When I try to move inside the building or into the school, I just hit the wall and stay there. I can't move past the bricks."

9.

Mattie prowled the halls of the school, a cage-spell ready in her mind. The plan was to fling the spell at Shezza as soon as the escaped prisoner showed herself.

Of course, the likelihood that Shezza would show herself, as opposed to lurking out of sight and killing or capturing Mattie first was pretty low. Her eyes, in seer mode, showed her an overlay of the near future against the view of the present, but Shezza would be expecting that and Mattie just knew that the devious bitch had a way to counter it.

Hearing footsteps behind her, she spun around, then relaxed when she realized it was her assigned partner, Sister Helen.

"Rooms 121-131 are clear," Sister Helen reported.

The two of them had decided that their best strategy would be for the nun to check the rooms while Mattie patrolled the hall outside, covering both bases in case Shezza tried to slip out of a classroom in advance of them.

Mattie nodded and they fell into the formation they'd been using as they progressed – Mattie clinging to the left side wall, Sister Helen to the right, with their arms outstretched to trip any spells that might be set anywhere along the way.

In theory, Mattie should be able to see any spells in seer mode, but they weren't taking any of the standard rules for granted when it came to Agent Shezza.

As she reached the next block of rooms, Mattie moved into position in the middle of the corridor, making way for Sister Helen to slip inside Room 132.

Mattie began to comb the hallway, step by step, on high alert for traps, intruders, and any other danger that might come her way.

Tillie's phone chirped, and she lunged for it. "It's Trevor!" she said.

Giovani looked up from the scrying stone, where he had been continuously trying to penetrate the magical wall surrounding the convent and school. "Does he know what's going on?"

Tillie shook her head. "He said he tried to call Mattie as soon as he got my message, but she's not answering his calls either."

Another text came through. "He's coming over."

"Good," said Giovani. "And then the three of us should head over there and see if we can help."

Sister Helen exited Room 132 and crossed the hall, glancing at Mattie first for the go-ahead.

Mattie had already checked the stretch of hallway between the two rooms, so she nodded an affirmative.

Sister Helen opened up the door to Room 133. "What on earth . . . ?"

Mattie drew the short sword she had strapped to her waist, but Sister Helen waved her hand, gesturing for her to replace it.

"What's going on?" Mattie asked. She turned off her seer sight, as it tended to confuse things when you were trying to have a conversation.

As soon as she did, she realized she could hear an odd beeping sound coming from the classroom.

Sister Helen didn't respond, just went into the room, so Mattie followed her.

"Huh." Mattie looked around. All of the classroom desks had been pushed to one side and in the center of the room, a mad-villain-esque computer bank had been set up on folding tables.

Bernie sat in the middle of it on a spinny desk chair, like a spider in a web, typing furiously on a keyboard and then pausing to stare up at one of the eight monitors surrounding him. Ignoring the two women, he whirled around in his chair to look at a different monitor, then pivoted back around to begin typing again.

Mattie cleared her throat.

"Yeah, yeah." Bernie neither looked up nor ceased his typing. "I know you're there. I hear Shezza's loose again. She's not here. You can go away and mark this room off your list."

Mattie grinned. "Noted. Thanks."

He lifted one hand from his keyboard to shoo them off, his other hand barely missing a beat as it flew across the entire range of keys.

Sister Helen raised an eyebrow at Mattie.

She shrugged in response and turned to leave.

"Wait!" said Bernie suddenly.

Mattie turned back, startled.

Bernie's hands stilled and he stared at one of his screens, an incredulous grin spreading across his face. He collapsed back in his chair and began to laugh.

Sister Helen glanced at Mattie again, her face alarmed, but Mattie just strode forward and then inched her way into

Bernie's circle through the one tiny opening, just large enough for her slender form.

"What is it?" she asked.

He stopped laughing and his brown eyes met hers. "I'm in," he whispered hoarsely. He cleared his throat. "I'm in," he repeated aloud. "I finally cracked it!"

Mattie glanced at the monitor directly in front of Bernie, which showed some kind of simplistic online forum. It looked completely innocuous to her, even a little bit old-fashioned, like the message boards she used in college to talk about movies.

"What am I looking at?" she asked. She stepped closer to the monitor, both to see it better and to make room for Sister Helen who was also trying to squeeze into the space.

"This is a top-secret message board the court's espionage department runs on the dark web!" Bernie exclaimed. "I suspected it existed and Polly and I–" his face darkened as he paused. He cleared his throat and continued. "Polly and I dug around for a long time looking for it. I found it a few months ago and have been working on hacking in ever since."

Sister Helen frowned. "But won't Shezza know–" She stopped and pressed her lips together.

Right. Shezza had been pretending to be Polly, so if Bernie had mentioned the forum at all in the time between when she killed Polly and when she was discovered, she could have taken down all of the important information.

But Bernie was shaking his head. His voice only shook a little bit as he explained. "By the time Shezza . . . took over, we had switched gears. We were focusing on getting into the financial accounts. Since we weren't working on this forum, it never came up in conversation."

"So, it's not compromised," Mattie breathed. She bent down to peer at the screen, reading aloud the messages at the top of the page. "Compte Serpent Rouge says, 'Le lapin est dans sa tanière. Où est le caméléon?'" She sighed. "Great. It's in French and in code."

"Well, of course it is," said Sister Helen. "You can't expect them to just leave their sensitive information on a hidden forum on the dark web where anyone can find it *and* make it easy to interpret."

Mattie grimaced. "Touche. So, who is the red snake and who is the bunny and where is the den?"

"It gets worse," said Bernie. "I don't even know what language the response is in."

Sister Helen tapped Mattie on the shoulder and she moved aside. The nun crouched down beside Bernie's chair. "Dutch. Roughly translated it says 'Chameleon missing, presumed captured. Please advise.'"

"You speak Dutch?" Mattie's eyebrows shot up.

"I speak and read twelve languages fluently and can get the gist of about thirty more." Sister Helen's voice was absent as she continued scanning the webpage in front of her. "I'm a WMT, but my specialty is linguistics."

Mattie frowned. Another acronym, similar to Sister Timothy Ann's. The WM was probably the same – warrior mage. "What's the T?"

Sister Helen glanced up at her. "Teacher," she said, her voice implying that everyone should know that.

Mattie looked at Bernie who shrugged back at her. "What's the WM?" he asked.

"Warrior mage, I guess," she said. "Sister Margaret said WMS was warrior mage scientist, about Sister Tim."

Sister Helen stood up. "I count seven different languages on this page alone," she said. "And it's clear that everyone using this forum has at least a basic command of each of them, as they're switching them up as they go back and forth. It would probably be an effective extra layer of confusion for most interlopers."

"Good thing we've got you," said Bernie with a grin.

She nodded. "Of course, I can't help with the meaning behind the translations. Luckily, the messages themselves are pretty basic."

Mattie nodded. "They probably figure they don't need to be particularly sophisticated since it's already so difficult to get into the forum to begin with."

"Hubris," said Bernie. "Gives us a bit of an edge, and heaven knows we could use it. We don't have much else going for us."

"Well," said Sister Helen, pulling her phone out of her pocket. "I'd better call in Sister Elaine to help with this; she can translate as well as I can and we need to get back to our search." She turned to Bernie. "You're doing good work. I'll send in another linguist for you."

Bernie opened his mouth as though to respond, then froze in place. His eyes rolled back into his head and he went limp, slumping forward in his chair.

10.

Tillie sipped tea from her travel mug, staving off a yawn, as Giovani turned his black SUV off the street and toward the parking lot behind St. Elizabeth Academy and Convent. The car stopped just short of entering the lot, and Giovani frowned, looking down at his feet.

"What's going on?" she asked.

"I'm not sure," he said.

"Why are we stopped?" Trevor leaned forward from the back seat.

Giovani hit the gas pedal harder and the tires squealed as the car tried futilely to move. "It's some kind of shield," he said. He put the car into park and turned off the ignition. "Let's go around and try the front door."

Tillie hopped out of the car, still clutching her tea and glancing around at her surroundings. It was still the middle of the night, and this was not a great neighborhood. Granted, anyone trying to mug a group of mages always got a nasty surprise, but it was still best to avoid the conflict altogether. She waited until Trevor and Giovani came around to her side and then put an invisibility shield around the three of them.

Trevor raised an eyebrow at her glowing hands. "Sight shield?"

"Yes, so stay close, please. I'd rather keep it as small as I can."

They walked in a tight cluster around the corner to the front steps and then stopped short as the same barrier blocked them. It was a weird feeling, walking up against the shield – it wasn't firm, like a wall, but squishy like invisible memory foam, gently but inexorably rebuffing them.

"You know what must have happened," said Trevor. "Shezza got out again and this is that damn security system. Very effective, but inconvenient for anyone trying to get in to help out."

"Maybe they can let us in if they know we're here," said Tillie.

"How?" said Giovani. "We can't get up to the building to knock or ring the bell, and no one is answering their phones."

"Who have you tried?" asked Trevor.

Tillie counted off on her fingers. "Mattie, Nicole, and Sister Margaret are the only numbers I have. Giovani tried Lisa, Kyle, and Jenn."

"None of the other nuns?" asked Trevor. He pulled his phone out of his pocket. "I took the liberty of grabbing the full roster of phone numbers from Sister Catherine, just in case anything like this happened."

Tillie grinned at him. "Look at you, being prepared! I'd almost mistake you for a seer!"

Trevor smiled back and shrugged modestly. "Aww, you're just saying that." He tried the first number on his list, putting it on speaker so they could all hear it.

After a minute, Sister Catherine's voice replaced the ringing. "Hello, this is Sister Catherine of the order of Saint Joan of Arc. I am unavailable right now, but–"

Trevor hung up and tried the next number. Sister Regina's voicemail message came on immediately and he hung up again.

Tillie held her breath as he hit Sister Helen's name and then the call icon. It rang a couple of times.

Mattie leaped forward, her fingers reaching for Bernie's pulse, which jumped strongly. She breathed a sigh of relief and turned around to enlist Sister Helen's assistance.

Unfortunately, Sister Helen had fallen into a heap on the floor behind her.

"Fuck!" Mattie crouched down beside the nun. "What the hell is going on here?" She ascertained that Sister Helen was also still alive and her gaze darted back and forth between her two fallen companions.

Biting her lip, she considered her options. "I guess it depends on who the fuck else just fainted," she mused aloud.

Pushing one of the computer desks aside with her shoulder – carefully, so nothing tipped over – Mattie gripped Sister Helen under her arms and tugged her out of the circle, laying her down, stretched out on the floor, in what she hoped was a relatively comfortable position.

Then she piled a couple of the keyboards on top of another to make room to rest Bernie's head on the desk in front of him.

She was just about to head out of the room to go find Sister Margaret, when a phone started ringing.

Mattie patted her pockets, but quickly realized the sound was coming from Sister Helen's supine figure. She gingerly extracted the phone from Sister Helen's breast pocket – what would happen to you if you accidentally groped a nun? – and hit the answer icon.

"Hello?"

"Sister Helen?" asked a familiar baritone.

"Trevor!" she said. "No, it's me."

"Matts!" said Trevor. "What's going on in there? We can't get in."

"Yeah, you wouldn't be able to," she said. "Shezza's on the loose again, the sneaky little bastard."

"We figured it was something like that," said her sister's voice. They must have her on speaker. "Can't someone let us in? We'd like to help."

"I don't know," said Mattie, grimly. She stepped over Sister Helen and headed toward the door as she spoke. "It actually just got a little more complicated."

As she headed down to the sub basement, where she knew Sister Margaret was supposed to be spearheading her own team, she related what had just happened, starting with Bernie's breakthrough and ending with the collapse of her two companions.

"So, I'm going to try and join up with anyone else who is awake, and I'll call you back when I figure out what the hell is going on and what the hell I can do about it," she concluded. She hung up the phone without waiting for a response and jogged down the last couple of stairs, barely pausing as she crashed through the double doors into the secret level that housed the detention cells – quite different from the detention rooms the high school students used upstairs – and the security systems, interrogation rooms, sparring studios, and any other rooms needed by an order of warrior mages.

Mattie slowed down now as she began peering into the minimum security observation cells housed on this hallway. Then she heard a sound from around the corner and sprinted down the hall toward it, just in time to see Sister Margaret exiting a cell.

Sister Margaret whirled toward her, drawing her twin swords gracefully as she did so, and then relaxing and resheathing them in a smooth movement as she caught sight of Mattie.

Mattie slid to a halt a safe distance away, wary of any other weapons her friend might have on her. "You're awake!" she said.

Sister Margaret's eyebrows shot up. "So, there are others who aren't?"

"Yeah." Mattie looked around for Sister Margaret's partner. "Sister Regina?"

Jerking her head toward the cell she'd just come out of, Sister Margaret replied, "Yep. Sister Helen?"

Mattie nodded. "And Bernie too. My sister and Trevor are outside, wondering if we can let them in."

Sister Margaret nodded. "That we can do. I'll be glad to have a few more people awake while we figure this out." She glanced at Mattie's hand. "That looks like one of our phones."

"Oh, right." She'd forgotten she still held it. "Sister Helen's. Trevor called it. I guess I left mine back in my room."

Sister Margaret began to walk and Mattie followed. "Excellent. While I fix the barrier to let in our friends, you get on the convent group chat and see if anyone responds to a roll call."

Mattie's steps slowed slightly as she examined the phone, swiping upward to see what would be needed to open it up. "Do you know the passcode?"

Sister Margaret paused. "Try 3745."

Mattie typed in the four numbers. "No."

"9023."

"No."

"Fuck." Sister Margaret stopped walking and chewed on her lower lip. "What is Sister Helen's code? I should know this."

"Should you?" Mattie raised her eyebrows.

"Yes! I know all of them, but Sister Helen and I work most closely together on security, and I should be most familiar with all of her codes. But which is for her phone?" She snapped her fingers. "I know. Do 6322."

Mattie typed it in and was rewarded with a page full of apps. "Got it."

"She just changed it," said Sister Margaret, setting off down the hall again. "I forgot."

Clicking on the text messaging app, Mattie looked for a group chat and found it immediately toward the top. As she walked after Sister Margaret, she typed in a message. *If you're awake, please check in.*

She looked up just in time to see Sister Margaret disappearing into a room she'd never been into. Following her in, she found herself surrounded once again by monitors, but this room made Bernie's set-up look like child's play.

Monitors were mounted on every surface of wall space in the large, windowless chamber, arranged in several bays around the room, each showing various areas on the grounds from all angles. In the center, there was a six-sided kiosk with a screen, keyboard, and some kind of scanner on each side.

And there were three nuns seated in front of various monitor banks, each of them slumped in her chair, draped over her desk, where she had clearly fallen unexpectedly asleep.

"It's like Sleeping Beauty's fucking tower in this place," Mattie muttered. "Except somehow I don't think these nuns are waiting for Prince Charming."

Sister Margaret pointed to the left side of the room. "You start there; I'll go to this end, and let's see if we can locate anyone else who's awake."

Despite the huge number of screens, it didn't take long to figure out that no one was moving on any of them. At this time of the night, most of the residents of the convent had been already asleep anyway; enough time had passed since the alarm going off that everyone who hadn't been conscripted for the search was back in their rooms.

All of those who had been searching – present company excluded – had fallen asleep mid-search, and Mattie spotted Sister Timothy Ann, Cardinal Neubacher, and another nun she didn't know asleep in a laboratory.

There was no sign of Agent Shezza anywhere, but that wasn't so surprising – the spy had to know they had cameras and was probably using a sight shield.

"All right, let's get the allies who aren't asleep in here to help us figure out why we escaped that fate," said Sister Margaret. She strode to the central kiosk and typed rapidly on one of the keyboards. She touched an indented spot on the screen's frame, presumably a fingerprint scanner, and then held still for the facial scan.

Next, she put her eye up to the retinal scanner and let it scan her eye both in and out of seer mode.

Finally, a robotic voice said, "Hello, Sister Margaret, Warrior Mage Protector. Please say the password in your normal voice."

"Fuck off you son of a bitch," said Sister Margaret.

"That is correct," said the robotic voice. "Please enter your command."

Mattie snickered. "Wasn't that already a command?"

Sister Margaret grinned. "I figured it was a password someone who actually knew me and might legitimately need to get in could figure out, but anyone trying to guess a password that a random nun would pick wouldn't guess it in a million years."

"You're a smart cookie," said Mattie.

Sister Margaret typed something into the computer. "All right, let's go. Text your sister and have her meet us at the front door."

11.

Tillie's phone beeped and she pulled it out of her pocket, pulling herself upright from her position leaning against the shield, which was actually quite comfy. "Mattie and Sister Margaret are on their way."

"Finally," said Giovani. "If I don't get some action, I'm going to fall asleep on my feet."

Trevor nudged Tillie and waggled his eyebrows. "You could give him some action," he murmured, just loud enough for her to hear.

She rolled her eyes. For an aro-ace guy, he was always awfully interested in her sex life. "I'm trying to keep things professional," she murmured back.

He grinned. "How is that not professional for you?"

"I'm retired!" Her voice rose indignantly.

Giovani glanced at them. "What?"

Tillie could feel her face turning beet red and she forced herself to take a deep, even breath to calm down her blood flow. "Nothing," she said through her teeth. "Don't worry about it."

Giovani glanced from her to Trevor and back. "Okay…."

She gave him her perkiest smile. "Trevor can be a real dick sometimes. Did you know that?"

Trevor laughed. "And now she's going to tell you all about what I did at our junior prom in high school to break up her and Peter Morgan, but the fact is that she started it, because she was supposed to be going to the dance with me, as my date–"

"Peter Morgan was my boyfriend!" said Tillie, narrowing her eyes. How, after all these years, did Trevor still think this behavior was justified? "He was gracious enough to–"

"No, no, no! It's not gracious when you–"

"You had plenty of other–" Tillie stopped and sighed as the front door opened and Sister Margaret called down to them.

"Hurry! You have eight seconds to get up the steps and into the building before it closes back up!"

Tillie trotted up the steps right on Giovani's heels, Trevor following closely behind her.

Just as she cleared the front door, she saw a blurry figure coming straight toward her, rushing past Mattie and Sister Margaret.

"It's Shezza!" Mattie cried out.

"Grab her!" yelled Sister Margaret.

Tillie flung her arms out to either side and Giovani grabbed her right hand, Trevor taking the left.

The front door slammed behind them as Agent Shezza crashed into their arms.

Time seemed to slow down as Mattie watched Agent Shezza fly past her toward the door. She cried out a warning and was gratified to see her sister and friends respond immediately, clasping hands like in the children's game Red Rover.

Astonishingly, it worked. Shezza collided with Tillie and Giovani's hands, and the line bent, but didn't break.

Mattie remembered her cage spell and reformed it in her mind, throwing it toward their twice-escaped prisoner.

Too late, she realized that she had also trapped Tillie inside.

Agent Shezza's face was a picture of pure rage as she shouted a Latin phrase and a flash of lightning emerged from her fingertips, aimed straight at Tillie's head.

"No!" Mattie shouted.

As Tillie fell, Mattie moved her fingers into a stitch, moving the first heavy object she laid eyes upon – a bust of some saint or other – directly over Shezza's head and dropping it.

The woman collapsed onto the floor beside Tillie, and Mattie released the cage spell.

By the time she got to Tillie, Giovani was already kneeling beside her, fingers at the side of her neck.

He looked up. "She's alive."

Mattie's breath released in a whoosh of pure relief. She'd already failed Ida this week. She didn't know what she'd do if–

She shoved the thought out of her head. No sense in dwelling on things that hadn't happened. She nodded toward Shezza. "What about her?"

Trevor was already reaching for the spy. He grabbed her wrist. "Yep. Also still among us."

That one Mattie could go either way on. She certainly wouldn't shed any tears over the woman, but on the other hand, maybe they could still get some information out of her.

"Good," said Sister Margaret. "Let's get her down to a supermax cell. Then we need to figure out why the hell everyone else is unconscious."

"What?" Trevor frowned at her.

Oh, right. They only knew about the escapee.

"More issues have come up," Mattie informed him.

"Of course they have." Giovani ran a hand over his sandy hair and let out a long, weary sigh that just about summed up everyone's state of mind.

Nobody said anything for a moment and then Giovani began to laugh, a high-pitched titter with little to no mirth in it.

Mattie froze and stared at him.

He had abandoned his beige suits and was dressed more like Trevor usually did. In fact, the clothes didn't quite fit him right, and she found herself wondering if they actually were Trevor's. His hair was standing on end from his newly acquired habit of running his hands through it, and his light brown eyes had a crazed light behind them.

As he continued giggling, he stumbled slightly and put out a hand to steady himself against the wall.

Nobody else moved; Trevor and Sister Margaret seemed just as transfixed as Mattie.

Finally, after what must have been a full minute of manic laughter, Giovani gradually quieted, and after one last snort, tears now running down his cheeks, he pushed himself away from the wall to stand upright.

He reached for his neck as though to straighten a tie, but must have realized he wasn't wearing one, so he ran his hands through his hair again instead. Then he took in a deep breath and released it quickly. "Wow. I needed that. I feel a lot better."

Oddly enough, he looked a lot better too.

Mattie studied the former Auditor agent and realized that he looked more relaxed than he had in the entire time she'd known him. "That was just building up inside you this whole time?"

"Oh, very much so," he said. "I should just crazy-laugh more often."

"Maybe we all should," said Sister Margaret. She gestured to Agent Shezza. "Later. Shall we? Before she comes to?"

Mattie turned her focus back to the task at hand, forming two spells in her mind and sending them toward Shezza, one to levitate her for easy transport, and one to freeze her muscles in case she woke up while they were moving her. She would have preferred to stitch her, but she didn't know which cell Sister Margaret had in mind, and she definitely didn't want to put her in anything but the most secure spot.

Sister Margaret turned to Trevor and Giovani. "We'll take care of Shezza. You two get Tillie someplace comfy and we'll meet you there."

Trevor nodded toward a nearby door. "Chapel atrium?"

"Perfect." Sister Margaret gestured to Mattie. "Follow me."

Tillie sat up, disoriented. Why was she lying on a couch in a vaguely familiar room, and why did her head hurt, and were Trevor and Giovani huddled over her, staring with those worried expressions?

Best to just ask. "Why am I lying on a couch in a vaguely familiar room and why does my head hurt, and why are you two huddled over me, staring with those worried expressions?"

Trevor's lips twitched. "I don't think anyone else would have asked that exact question, and I don't think you could have asked anything else."

"Just answer it." She waved them aside and they stepped back, Giovani moving around to her side to help her as she struggled to sit up.

"This vaguely familiar room is the atrium of the chapel at St. Elizabeth's," said Trevor. "You're here and you hurt and we're worried because Agent Shezza knocked you out with a spell. No one else is here and worried, because most of them are asleep, probably knocked out with a different Agent Shezza spell, although that is unconfirmed as of this time. It appears that Mattie and Sister Margaret are the only ones who were here and were not affected, and they are currently engaged in putting Shezza into a new cell, from which she will hopefully be unable to break out."

Tillie frowned. "How did they manage that?"

Trevor paused. "Which?"

"Why aren't they asleep?"

"We're not sure," said Giovani. "That's our next puzzle to figure out."

She studied Giovani. "You look better somehow."

He grinned. "Thanks. I think I managed to get some of the crazies out. For now."

"Oh, good." She leaned back and then frowned and turned back to Trevor. "What do you mean, 'which?'"

"I just wasn't sure if you were asking about the sleepy spell or how they found a cell Shezza couldn't break out of."

"Oh." She thought about it for a moment. "She wasn't in a super secure cell to begin with, was she? I mean, she was well-guarded, but she's sneaky. That was a mistake."

Trevor shrugged. "Nothing we can do about it now except not make the same mistake again."

Tillie's eyebrows shot up. "Since when do you not obsess over past mistakes?"

Giovani interrupted. "Presumably since he started learning magery and working on spells alongside of stitching."

"Huh." Tillie cocked her head at Trevor. "I didn't even know you were working on spells. What about seeing?"

Trevor shrugged. "Not yet. I'd like to eventually, but it seems better not to divide my focus too much, don't you think?"

Tillie thought about how neither she nor Giovani had been able to get a real bead on what was actually happening here, only a vague premonition. Morphing in all directions had weakened their natural talents to a noticeable detriment. "You're probably right."

"Of course I'm right," said Trevor firmly. "How does your head feel?"

Tillie moved her head around a bit, experimentally. "Better but not best."

"That will have to do," said Sister Margaret, striding into the room.

Mattie rushed past her and straight to Tillie's side. "You're awake! Are you okay? How do you feel?"

"Better but not best," Tillie repeated. She shrugged. "My head's a little sore, but I think I'll live."

"Glad to hear it." Mattie sat on the edge of her couch, taking her hand and squeezing it a little. "Did the guys fill you in on the whole shebang?"

Tillie nodded. "I'm a little unclear on the whole sleeping spell situation. Do you think you could walk me through it?"

Sister Margaret sighed. "We're all a little unclear on that. We had two separate groups of people on the property – the nuns who live here and a small group of former Auditor agents who are staying here right now – all of whom succumbed to this spell, except for one of each."

"That's not entirely true," said Giovani. "Mattie was never an Auditor. So that might explain why she isn't asleep."

"And what about Cardinal Neubacher?" Mattie pointed out. "He's not a nun, but he's asleep."

"Interesting point," said Sister Margaret. She rubbed a finger up and down on the bridge of her nose. "These kinds of puzzles really aren't my strong suit, to be honest."

Tillie smiled. "Well, of course not; they're no seer's strong suit." She turned to Trevor and gestured him forward. "Trevor? Would you like to take the reins here?"

Trevor's face lit up – he had always loved this kind of thing. His fingers moved and they glowed momentarily as a large free-standing chalkboard appeared beside him. He picked up the chalk that sat on the ledge underneath it and began to write.

"Okay, so let's say that the main group of people is the nuns, right? What else do they have in common besides nunhood, because if it was just nunhood, Sister Margaret would also be asleep, right?"

Mattie perked up as Trevor wrote *sleeping nuns* on the blackboard. Tillie made fun of them for it, but she and Trevor had always loved puzzles. "And what does Cardinal Neubacher have in common with them that Sister Margaret doesn't?"

Trevor pointed to Mattie. "Yes!" He wrote *Cardinal* and *former Auditors.* "This seems like a very diverse group we've got here, but they must have things in common."

"They're all mages," said Mattie.

"But so are you and Sister Margaret," pointed out Tillie.

Trevor moved to the other side of the blackboard and wrote *Mattie* and *Sister Margaret*, then wrote *mages* under both sides.

"Cardinal Neubacher and all of the nuns in this order are Warrior Mages," said Sister Margaret.

Trevor cocked his head and studied Sister Margaret. "I would consider the former agents warriors too, but I'm sensing that's some kind of title."

"Yeah, I've been hearing that a lot today. Tonight. Whatever this is," said Mattie. "What does that mean?"

"It's a designation," said Sister Margaret. "We use it among the mages who either have taken vows or work in certain positions for the Vatican. There are Warrior Mages and Scholar Mages and then beyond that there are the specialties – many of the nuns here are WMT's, which is Warrior Mage Teachers. And then they have a specialty beyond that. A couple others put their specialty first and are teachers secondarily – Sister Tim, for example, is a WMS, a Warrior Mage Scientist, specifically a chemist, and while she does teach chemistry at the high school, she only teaches the very advanced classes, because her focus is on doing research for the order and for the Vatican."

"But you don't teach here, do you?" said Mattie. "What is your designation?"

"WMP," she responded. "I'm a Warrior Mage Protector."

"Are you the only WMP here?" asked Trevor. He leaned forward, his eyes shining.

"Yes!" Sister Margaret jumped up and unzipped the armor on her left arm, showing them a large tattoo of a stylized shield, in a similar style to the sword Mattie knew decorated the nun's other arm. "This has all kinds of protection spells woven into it; I got it at my induction ceremony when I was promoted to Protector."

"So, that tattoo might have armored you against this sleeping spell?" said Giovani. "That would make sense, if it was an umbrella kind of thing; I don't know much about those spells, but just talking to Amy earlier, she made it sound like the ones she's aware of are very basic."

"So, what if we have two spells here?" suggested Mattie. "One that targets WM's, but doesn't account for a WMP's extra shields, and one that targets the former Auditors. It's pretty naive of us to assume that the black-eye spell is the only one the court put into place, just waiting for activation."

"So, if that's the case, we should be able to wake up the former Auditors in the same way we dispelled the last one," said Giovani. "And it looks like it was only activated on the people who were actually present, since I'm unaffected."

"Which makes sense if Shezza activated it as a distraction!" Mattie leapt to her feet. "Did we totally just figure this thing out?"

Trevor smiled at her. "We have a working theory that makes a lot of sense," he chided, gently. "Let's not celebrate until we know for sure, and can break it. And even if this is correct, we don't know if we can break the spell on the Warrior Mages in the same way, right?"

Mattie deflated. "Yeah, yeah, you're right."

She whirled around as Sister Margaret's cell phone began to ring. "Huh," said Sister Margaret. She answered it and hit the speaker icon.

Sister Catherine's voice filled the room. "--you have any idea what's going on around here, Sister? I was searching for Shezza, and then suddenly I woke up, like I had been knocked out, I've got a dozen others claiming the same thing happened to them, and we all have a text from Sister Helen asking us to check in, but when we did, there was no response from her, and what's more, I found Sister Helen and she is similarly disoriented and doesn't have her phone on her."

"How long have you been awake?" Sister Margaret demanded.

"Did Bernie and the others wake up too?" asked Mattie at the same time.

Without waiting for a response, Mattie pulled out Sister Helen's phone and saw, sure enough, a whole bunch of text notifications. She must have accidentally set the thing to silent mode somehow.

"Looks like these texts came in about ten minutes ago," she said.

"Who is that?" asked Sister Catherine. "Where are you?"

"Hi, Sister Catherine; it's Mattie." She stepped closer to Sister Margaret's phone and leaned close to speak into it. "I have Sister Helen's phone; it started ringing just after she fell asleep, and since I was awake, I answered it. I sent that text at Sister Margaret's request."

"We're in the chapel," Sister Margaret interrupted. "Let's all meet here and discuss our next move."

12.

As nuns and former Auditor agents – apparently they all woke up at the same time – began to filter through the atrium and into the chapel itself, Tillie swung her legs off the couch and braced herself to stand up and follow them.

Giovani and Trevor each took one of her arms to support her, and her lips twitched. In her old life as an escort, she had occasionally been one of two women on some rich idiot's arms at some major event or other. What did it say about the twist her existence had taken, that she was now being escorted by two not-so-eligible bachelors into the chapel of a high school for an impromptu meeting that consisted mostly of nuns?

Honestly, it was too bizarre to really even contemplate.

"I'm fine, guys," she said. "I can walk on my own. Even my headache is almost gone."

That was another strange thing. Shezza was powerful and had hit her at point blank range with a lightning spell. Why was she walking around with ease so soon? What kind of game was Shezza playing? Had she held back? Or was she just that sapped of energy?

Maybe this runaround had taken a toll on the great Agent Shezza. Something worth pondering.

Tillie led Trevor and Giovani up to the front of the room, where Mattie was already seated beside Sister Margaret.

Sliding onto the not-terribly-comfortable bench, Tillie listened as Sister Margaret explained the whole Warrior Mage thing to Mattie in more depth. Her sister seemed oddly curious about it, for someone who had never shown any interest in religion before. Was her staunchly agnostic twin considering taking vows as a nun, just to become a Warrior Mage Something?

"And you mentioned that not all of the people who bear these designations are nuns, right?" Mattie asked.

Maybe not.

"That's right," said Sister Margaret. "There are a lot of laypersons who work for the Vatican, and at one point in history they would have been required to take vows, but this is the 21st century, and frankly not a lot of people are lining up to dedicate their lives to Christ anymore."

"Do you have to be Catholic?" said Mattie.

Sister Margaret shrugged. "I would think it probably helps. Wait, are you considering working for the Church?"

Mattie echoed her shrug. "Maybe. It's not that big of a stretch to go from working in a Catholic high school to working as some kind of warrior for the Church, is it?"

"Actually–"

Sister Margaret was interrupted by Sister Catherine, who stood in the space between the audience and the steps that went up to the altar-thingy – Tillie really wasn't up on the terminology. Was it called an altar? That's what she called the one in her ritual room at home, which looked very similar.

"Thank you for gathering – again," Sister Catherine was saying with a small, strained smile. "I know this has been a strange and eventful night, and it's basically morning now. I'd like to get everyone up to speed at once to avoid any repetition or confusion."

A loud buzzing sound filled the room, coming from the open doors at the back.

Tillie twisted around, looking for the source.

"Oh, what the fuck now?" said Sister Margaret. "It's five o'fucking clock in the motherfucking morning and someone is ringing the fucking school doorbell? Why? WHY?"

Sister Catherine sighed. "Sister Margaret, please. I know we're all stressed out, but do you think you could rein in the swearing in this sacred space at least?"

Sister Margaret bowed her head, took in a deep breath and released it, then looked up again. "Yes. I'm sorry, Sister."

Sister Catherine nodded her acknowledgement. "Let's see. Mattie? Trevor? I believe you're already up to speed on this – would you mind seeing who is at the door?"

Mattie peeked her head around the door leading from the chapel atrium into the building's lobby, hoping to catch a glimpse of whoever was outside before they saw her.

The sun was just starting to peek its own head up, and the dawn light revealed three shadowy figures skulking on the front stoop. Then again, any figure was going to be shadowy and look skulky at this time of the morning, so that probably wasn't much to go on.

"Do you recognize any of them?" Trevor murmured, his own head peering just over hers.

"Nuh huh," said Mattie. She could barely make out their faces, though. "Might as well just go talk to them."

Decision made, she strode out into the open, and the three figures stopped skulking and jumped to attention, watching her as she made her way over to the complicated intercom box and looked for a button that would let her talk to them without actually opening the door.

"It's that one in the corner," said Trevor, pointing to a square white button without any numbers next to it. "Not the black one – that unlocks it."

"Thanks." Mattie pushed the button and spoke into the box. "Um. Yes?"

One of the men responded, but she couldn't hear anything through the door.

Trevor gently pushed her aside and held down the white button. "You're going to have to hit the button on your side too."

The man looked around.

"Over there." He pointed to a similar box off to the side and the guy walked over to it and examined it.

"The square white button. Yeah, the one at the bottom."

The man pressed the button and spoke into the box. "I'm looking for someone. Is former Auditor Agent Garaveldi here? Or Agent Nicole Poe?"

Mattie frowned. These guys didn't really look like Auditors – they were wearing identical black suits and looked more like FBI agents than anyone from the organization they were fighting.

But she still felt uneasy about identifying Giovani. Or Nicole, if she was even present. "This is a Catholic high school," she hedged. At least that way if these people turned out to be someone they would end up working with later, she hadn't lied to them.

The man's lips twisted. "That really does sidestep the question very neatly, doesn't it?"

Okay, so he wasn't an idiot. That didn't really make her feel any better. Best to play dumb a little longer and hope they let some information slip before she did. "I'm afraid I don't understand the question. You're looking for some kind of tax auditor? An IRS agent?"

The man studied her before hitting the button again. "Which one are you? You're one of those red-headed twins, right? Mathilda Christmas or something?"

Mattie took a step back before she could stop herself. How the hell did this guy know who she was? Sort of know who she was, anyway. That was really too close for comfort.

Pulling herself together, she stepped back up to the intercom and hit the button. "Okay, let's stop pussyfooting around here. You don't get to ask any more questions and I'm not going to give you any more information until I get some out of you. You show up here, basically in the middle of the night, looking for a high-ranking member of our . . ." she paused. What were they exactly? An army? No. "–organization, knowing things you have no business knowing, and you're expecting me to just answer your questions? Absolutely not. Let's start with your names."

"Fair enough." He gestured toward himself. "I'm Ford McEntire, formerly Agent McEntire of the Auditor organization." He indicated his two companions. "This is James Freeman and Mike Lansdowne. Also former Auditor agents."

Mattie exchanged a shocked glance with Trevor. There were other former agents out there? How had they escaped being hunted down by the organization?

Ford continued. "We're part of a group called the Harpers, made entirely of former agents and court members who have escaped the clutches of the organization, and we need your help."

13.

Tillie listened as Sister Catherine ran through the events of the past couple of hours – Shezza escaping, the small group designated to break into pairs to find her.

A murmur ran through the crowd when she reached the part about Bernie hacking into the dark web forum used by the court's spies.

"I will now yield the floor to the hacker himself," said Sister Catherine, stepping aside as Bernie jogged forward, dressed in his characteristic rockabilly jeans and white t-shirt with the sleeve rolled up around what Tillie knew were actually drugged darts, rather than the traditional cigarettes.

"Thank you, Sister," said Bernie in his southern drawl. "This is a very exciting win, as it appears that this message board is active and used by multiple agents with animal code names. We've only done some preliminary analysis of the contents of the board, but we think that our own captive Shezza may be known by the designation Chameleon, and it appears that the organization is currently looking for her. The forum uses a wide range of languages, and I am hoping to get some volunteers among the linguistically-inclined sisters to help me out with the decoding."

A trio of hands raised and Sister Catherine moved back to center stage. "Sisters Helen, Elaine, and Roberta. Thank you."

The three nuns stood up and followed Bernie as he strode down the aisle and out of the chapel.

Sister Catherine continued. "Directly after this breakthrough is when everyone in the building except for Sister Margaret and Mattie apparently keeled over into a deep sleep.
They, with the help of Tillie, Trevor, and Giovani, who arrived shortly thereafter, following a hunch, apprehended Agent Shezza and put her in a maximum security cell. At that point, Sister Margaret disabled the barrier spell. We believe that Shezza had somehow tied her sleep spell to the barrier spell, and since it is keyed to all of us in the building, that sent the entire order to sleep. She must have also tied it to another pre-set spell on anyone in the building who had one leftover from their time as Auditor agents. We are unsure at this point if it managed to ensnare Cardinal Neubacher because he is a fellow WM or by some other mechanism, but either way, once the barrier spell was disabled, so was the spell over us. We also believe that Sister Margaret's Protectorate tattoo shielded her from it."

She paused. "Our next step will be dealing with Agent Shezza. To that end, I yield the floor to Sister Timothy Ann."

Sister Catherine stepped aside as a plump gray-haired nun stood and walked slowly up to the front, amidst a scattering of tired applause. She pushed her glasses up her nose and smiled widely, her eyes sparkling with excitement. "I know you're all exhausted, so I'll try to keep this brief, even though I personally want to be jumping up and down."

Tillie straightened in her seat. She knew Sister Timothy Ann as a kind, mild-mannered, but rather boring woman. It was always interesting when such a person stopped being boring and got excited about something.

"Many of you know that I've been working on some old formulas found in one of those out-of-way archives the WML's like to discover every so often. These are the best kind of puzzles, in my opinion – part science, part magery, but also could just be alchemical nonsense. Fun for the whole family."

Tillie joined several people in chuckling at that, even as she wondered what a WML was. . . . It involved archives; Warrior Mage Librarian, maybe? That was an intriguing combination.

"One of these formulas was labeled as a truth serum, which is all very Hollywood but could have exciting implications for ye olde WMI's like the Cardinal here." She gestured toward Cardinal Neubacher, who inclined his head regally, a small smile playing at his lips. Sister Timothy Ann paused dramatically. "Especially since they're a bit more constrained than the Inquisitors were in days of yore."

Tillie was startled at the hearty laugh that got from most of the nuns. Torture humor? Kind of macabre, but who was she to judge?

Sister Tim beckoned and a dark-skinned woman wearing jeans and a flannel shirt who looked to be about Tillie's age came forward, carrying a small folding table and a medical bag. She began to set up the table and pull various items from the bag, laying them out on the table's surface.

Another nun, her hands glowing with some kind of spell, followed with a folding chair. She set up the chair and then hurried back out of the room.

She returned a moment later, she and Sister Margaret tugging a subdued Shezza down the center aisle toward the front of the chapel.

Shezza was very subdued indeed – her wrists were handcuffed together, her ankles shackled. She also seemed to be in a stasis spell and she was levitated a couple inches off the ground, and her two escorts guided her easily using cords attached to the handcuffs.

The trio reached Sister Timothy Ann and her assistant, and Sister Tim gestured toward the chair.

The speller nun's glowing hands pulsed once and then stopped glowing, as first the levitation spell and then the stasis spell dropped from Shezza.

The prisoner rolled her neck, looking around with interest, but not speaking or making any attempt at escape.

"Please, sit down," said Sister Timothy Ann.

Shezza craned her neck to see the chair behind her, and then dropped into it, awkwardly shuffling her feet and placing her bound hands on her lap.

Sister Margaret and the speller stood beside her, ready to act if she moved in any way they didn't like.

"And now," said Sister Timothy Ann with a flourish, "my assistant, the lovely Sister Mary Elizabeth–" The flannel-clad nun bowed. "–will administer the serum."

Sister Mary Elizabeth picked up a syringe and loaded it up. She held up the needle dramatically to appreciative oooohs and aaaahhs from the audience.

Tillie was a bit nonplussed by the theatrics of the whole thing. Truth serum was technically considered torture, right? She was pretty sure she'd read that it was banned in a lot of countries. Then again, the article she'd read had said that truth serums were completely ineffective and were basically just roofies, so maybe it wasn't considered torture if it really worked and wasn't simply an excuse to drug and disorient someone.

And since this one had magery behind it, maybe it really did work.

Tillie leaned forward as Sister Mary Elizabeth injected the serum into Shezza's arm, efficiently swapping it for a cotton ball as she slid the needle back out. She bandaged up the injection site with practiced movements and then stepped back.

"It does take a few minutes to take effect," said Sister Tim. "While we wait, I'll explain a little about how it works. As I'm sure you're aware, pure science has never developed a serum or drug that has actually and consistently compelled anyone to tell the truth. As far as we know, neither has any mage, but of course magery is so subjective and varied that it's difficult to keep tabs on who can do what, outside of the very basics."

A murmur of agreement ran through the crowd.

"There have been certain drugs developed, of course, that come close to being truth serums – drugs that make the recipient more suggestible, more likely to talk, and less likely to resist answering questions, but like torture, these have been found to be unreliable at best for gathering any actual intel.

"The book I've been working with dates from the late Medieval period, and Sister Helen has been gracious enough to help me puzzle through the Elizabethan English. The drug they suggested using is complete nonsense, although it made a quite tasty herbal tea."

Tillie smiled.

"But the magery they used was ingenious. And combined with a blend of modern drugs, including midazolam, amobarbital, and just a teensy bit of rohypnol, we have what I believe is an actual truth serum that can be used effectively on anyone. The magery requires a speller, a stitcher, and someone who can morph with spells and seeing together, so it was quite complicated to get it all put together. We have spells and stitches placed on the serum itself and the syringe that administers it."

Sister Timothy Ann glanced at Shezza, who was beginning to sway slightly, her eyes glassy.

"I think we may be ready to show you how it works," said Sister Tim, smiling. "I suggest anyone who has seer capabilities switch over to that mode so you can really see what's happening here. Everyone else, you'll still get a good show. Cardinal?" She beckoned to Cardinal Neubacher, who stood and began making his way to the front of the room.

Tillie blinked into seer mode and was unsurprised to see a murky miasma hanging over Shezza, similar to what she was used to seeing on someone who was drunk or high. She noted that there were glowing threads woven into the mist and sparkling dots as well – presumably the result of the spells and stitches used.

"The serum works in two ways," Sister Timothy Ann continued. "If the subject is trying not to answer, it will force them to do so anyway. And if the subject is trying to lie, they will be unable to do so."

Looking at Shezza, Tillie saw a hint of yellow coloring the woman's aura – the color of fear. Maybe this counted as torture after all. Then again, Shezza wouldn't even hesitate to do the same to any of them.

As Cardinal Neubacher reached the front, Sister Tim stepped back, ceding the floor to him. Sister Margaret and the other guarding nun remained in place, ready for any trouble that might arise.

Tillie doubted Shezza was capable of causing trouble at the moment. She was completely out of it.

"Hello, dear," said Cardinal Neubacher, in that creepy-compassionate way of his. "I'm going to ask you a few questions."

Why bother with the compassion schtick when she was drugged anyway? Maybe it was just habit; part of his process.

"What is your real name?" he asked.

Shezza's face twisted and contorted, as she clearly tried to keep her lips sealed. After a few seconds, she blurted out, "Chameleon." A horrified expression crossed her face and she clamped her lips shut once more, her eyes squeezing shut.

Tillie blinked. The woman's actual name was Chameleon?

Sister Timothy Ann stepped forward, lifting her arms to quell the rising murmur from the crowd. "The serum is interesting in that it does tend to default to more emotional responses rather than dry facts. Perhaps the question could be rephrased. 'Real' is a subjective term. Chameleon, which seems to be a code name, may be the name she identifies with the most."

"What is your legal name?" asked Cardinal Neubacher.

"I do not legally exist in any country," said Shezza, opening her eyes. Her voice was dull and flat, as though she'd given up fighting the serum. "I have three passports. The names on them are Teresa Shezza, Frieda Nielson, and Sarai Schmidt."

"What is the first name that was ever given to you?" Was that a hint of exasperation in Cardinal Neubacher's voice?

"Princess Madeleine Darlington," said Shezza.

Tillie inhaled sharply. Princess! So, she really was the daughter of the Pontiff.

"Thank you, Madeleine," said the Cardinal, his voice going gentle again. "See, it's a relief when you tell me the truth, isn't it? You don't have to hide your true self with me. Tell me, Madeleine, what is your role within the Auditor organization?"

Mattie moved aside as Trevor stepped forward and hit the intercom button. "You can understand our skepticism," he said. "This feels very abrupt and very much like something perfectly designed as a trap set by the Auditor organization itself."

"I do understand," said Ford. "This is, of course, the dilemma of every clandestine group. How can we ever know who is on our side and who is working for the other side? Especially in the world of magery, when there are so many different sides. Tell me, what can we do to show you we are who we say we are?"

Trevor glanced in Mattie's direction as though looking for guidance, but she had none to give. She shrugged broadly. The guy was right. What would they even accept as evidence? She held up a finger to the visitors and grabbed Trevor's arm, pulling him away from the glass door and turning so their backs were to it. If these people were spies, they could probably read lips, after all.

"He's right," said Trevor, echoing Mattie's thoughts. "What do we do here?"

"I don't think this is a decision we can make on our own," said Mattie. "Much as I like to think of myself as in charge, this affects our whole group. Plus, even if I did trust them, which I don't, I certainly wouldn't feel right letting someone in here without either Sister Catherine or Sister Margaret's approval."

"Fair point," said Trevor. He paused. "They asked for Giovani."

"Yeah, and Nicole. So?"

"It makes sense that they would ask for Nicole, since she's the leader of the Auditor rebel group," said Trevor. "She's not even here, but they wouldn't necessarily know that, since this has become kind of our base. But Giovani is here, and I'm wondering why they asked for him, and not, say Aaron or another long-standing member of that group."

Understanding dawned. "You're saying that if they're familiar with that splinter group from their time in the organization, it's odd that one of the people they asked for was never a member, and wasn't even aware of them until after he left."

Trevor nodded. "Which makes me wonder if they're asking after him because they knew him personally."

"And maybe he'd be able to vouch for them," said Mattie.

"It's worth a shot," said Trevor.

"Sure." Mattie chewed on her bottom lip for a moment. "Then again, if they're court and they just know about the Battle of St. Louis and the role Giovani played in it, maybe they're actually trying to find out if he and Nicole are here and get confirmation that they're still in leadership roles."

"So, if we go grab Giovani, we might be playing right into their hands." Trevor sighed, rubbing his temples. "So, what are we going to do here?"

"I guess it doesn't hurt to go ask Giovani if he knows any of these people, but don't tell them where we're going and don't bring out Giovani where they can see him, unless he says it's okay?"

"That makes sense." Trevor paused. "We should probably get other people involved too, huh? The nuns at least?"

"Well, they're all in one place anyway," Mattie pointed out. "So let's just go see if their meeting is at a good stopping point. If not, it can't hurt to let these guys languish for a bit anyway."

"Unless they really do need our help and it's urgent," Trevor pointed out.

"Oh, maybe we should ask them about that," suggested Mattie. "Might help with our final decision."

"Good point." Trevor turned around and strode back over to the doors, pressing the intercom button again. "You said you need our help. We're not saying that we trust you or that we'll help you, but what did you mean by that?"

"Sure, of course. I get that," said Ford. "We're being hunted by a team of Auditor agents."

Mattie elbowed Trevor aside to get to the button. "And you led them right here to us?" she demanded.

"No, no, of course not!" he said. He hesitated. "We're pretty sure we lost them. But if we went back to the rest of our group, we'd have been caught for sure. We have no idea if they know where our base is; they might have been lying in wait for us."

Trevor reached around Mattie, his face grim. "If they're agents and they're hunting you, they may be tracking you."

Ford shook his head. "We know how to cloak ourselves. And we'd be happy to teach you too, if you'd just give us sanctuary and help us take out these agents!"

Mattie hit the button. "We can't make this decision on our own. Stay here. We'll be back in–" she glanced at Trevor and he shrugged. "We'll be back when we can."

Agent Shezza – Madeleine – began to rattle off a long list of titles. "Princess of Intelligence, Duchess of Clandestine

Operations, Baroness of Special Agents, Countess of Secret Identities, Dame of the Order of the Owl, Third Heir to the Pontiff."

Tillie's lips twitched. What an absurdly pretentious litany. And they all seemed to mean the same thing – she was in charge of spies.

"So, you're in charge of the spies?" Cardinal Neubacher's clarification query echoed Tillie's thoughts.

"Yes," said Madeleine. "I direct all intelligence operations within the organization."

"And you take over as Pontiff if he and your two older siblings should perish?" said Cardinal Neubacher.

"No," said Madeleine.

There was a pause, and then the Cardinal prompted her. "How does the succession of the Pontiff work, then?"

"If the Pontiff dies, the inner circle of his advisors appoints a new one from their numbers," said Madeleine. "Usually after a long period of debate, duels, and a series of assassinations."

"So, in what way are you the third heir to the Pontiff, then?"

"Ceremonially," said Madeleine. "I would never want to be Pontiff anyway."

Tillie froze and a hush fell over the room. This felt very much like Madeleine was volunteering information. Nothing in Cardinal Neubacher's question would have compelled her to say that.

"So much backstabbing and posturing." Madeleine's voice was soft, but filled with a quiet anger. "What's the point of it all? So a petty little man can be in charge of a bunch of other petty little men and women? My father is miserable and he thinks he's happy because other people tell him he's important." She paused. "People tell me I'm important too. That doesn't make me happy."

Tillie waited with bated breath for Madeleine to continue, but she simply slumped in her chair.

"What would make you happy?" Cardinal Neubacher asked, gently.

Madeleine lifted her head. The room was completely silent for a moment, as her face twisted and contorted. Was she resisting the spell's compulsion to speak or was she emotion and unsure of what to say?

Finally she spoke. "A community. A real community of people who support each other instead of fighting. A family who enjoys being together and has each other's back, not just because they've been thrown in together, but because they want to help. I want to belong to someone who wants me to belong, for myself and not my skillset. I want to be myself and not Agent Shezza or Polly or Chameleon."

Tears pricked Tillie's eyes. This woman had never had any other option but to be a spy for the organization she'd been born into.

Tillie could only imagine the loneliness of a child born into a secret society and probably trained from a young age to be an operative. A child whose father, and maybe also her mother, had been focused only on getting ahead and gaining power. A child who had grown up into an adult so damaged and ruthless that she was constantly throwing herself into harm's way on behalf of her abusers.

Sister Margaret spoke up. Her voice was strong, but Tillie could see that her eyes were welling up as well. "If you found a community that accepted you, would you be willing to fight with them against the Pontiff?"

Madeleine didn't even hesitate. "Absolutely."

Sister Catherine stepped forward and laid a gentle hand on Cardinal Neubacher's arm. "I think we're done here."

He nodded and turned away from his prisoner. Tillie could see true pity in his face, an expression distinctly different from the faux compassion he had honed into a weapon for his inquisitions.

Sister Mary Elizabeth hurried back up to assist Madeleine to her feet. "I'll get her to the infirmary to sleep off the serum." Two other nuns stood to help as Sister Mary Elizabeth guided Madeleine toward the exit.

Tillie turned to watch them leave. As soon as they were gone, Mattie and Trevor burst into the room and headed straight for Sister Margaret, who still stood in front of the altar-area, deep in conversation with Cardinal Neubacher.

Mattie whispered urgently to Sister Margaret, gesturing toward the bench where Tillie sat beside Giovani.

Sister Margaret turned and beckoned them to come forward.

"Giovani!" said Mattie as they approached. "Good. Do you know a guy named Agent Ford McEntire?"

Giovani stopped walking, his posture tense, his eyes widening. "I'm not sure," he said, slowly. "I do know an Agent McEntire." He paused and then corrected himself. "Knew an Agent McEntire."

Mattie's eyebrows rose. "He's supposed to be dead?"

"That actually meshes," said Trevor. "If he faked his death, that might explain him being able to escape the organization, at least until now."

"What are you talking about?" asked Giovani, his voice strained. He ran his hands over his hair in the way he did when he was nervous – increasingly becoming a regular habit.

"What did Agent McEntire look like?" said Trevor.

"Dark red hair," said Giovani. "Pale skin with freckles all over his face. Kind of gangly."

Mattie nodded. "That's him, all right."

Giovani ran his hands over his hair again, taking in a deep breath and letting it out again. "What. Is. Going. On?" he asked through clenched teeth.

"Agent McEntire is outside, along with two other guys," said Mattie. "They're asking for you. They say they're escaped agents, they're with a group of more escaped agents, and they – just the three of them, if I understand them correctly – are being hunted by a team of current agents. They're asking for sanctuary."

"Do you trust Agent McEntire?" asked Sister Margaret.

Giovani closed his eyes. "I used to. I used to trust him with my life," he said. "Agent McEntire was my partner back when I was an agent. He died right in front of me, just a few months ago."

Into the silence that fell over their huddled group, Tillie could hear Sister Timothy Ann chattering excitedly with Cardinal Neubacher, extolling further applications of the truth serum and other formulas from the same ancient text.

"Does Sister Tim have any more of that truth serum?" she asked. "Might be a good time for another demonstration."

Trevor frowned. "Wait a second. Truth serums are not something to play around with. Most world governments won't allow it, and consider it torture. You're going to subject someone who was already traumatized by the Auditors and escaped to actual torture?"

"What do you mean, 'another demonstration?'" asked Mattie. "What's going on?"

Sister Margaret sighed. "He would be given a choice. We wouldn't just strap him down and poke him with a needle."

"It's not much of a choice if they're really running for their lives," Trevor argued. "Given the option between being drugged and being killed, a lot of people would choose the drugs, but that doesn't make it much less traumatic."

"Well, wait a second." Tillie raised her hand. "You didn't give Madeleine a choice. What makes these guys so different?"

"Who is Madeleine?" asked Mattie. "What the hell is going on?"

"Agent Shezz's real name is Madeleine," said Giovani.

"She'd better not go by Maddie," Mattie muttered. "Wait, did you guys truth serum Agent Shezza?"

Trevor threw his hands into the air. "I just want to go on record that I do not approve of this action at all. Truth serums aren't even effective."

"This one is," said Sister Margaret. "It's not just drugs – it uses magery to ensure that they can't resist answering, and they have to answer truthfully."

"You see how that's worse, though, right?" said Trevor. "That sounds so invasive and traumatizing."

Even though Tillie had thought the same beforehand, somehow she couldn't help but defend the actions she'd sat by and watched. "You think Shezza wouldn't have done the same to any of us?"

Trevor's eyes widened as he spun to face her head on. "You're okay with this?"

She shrugged, trying to present a nonchalant face. "It seems like an effective tool. It got us one new ally, and who knows how much damage Madeleine would have continued to inflict on us. Plus, now we know what's going on in her head, maybe we can help her begin to heal."

Mattie stamped her foot on the marble floor and shouted. "Will somebody please tell me what in the sam-fuck is going on?"

A shocked hush fell over the chapel as clusters of chattering nuns turned to stare at them.

Sister Margaret threw back her head and laughed heartily into the silence. She waved to the crowd to get back to their own business, and slowly, the gathered women turned back to their conversations.

"Come on," said Sister Margaret. "Let's go get set up in another room, and I'll tell you all about it on the way."

"Giovani should stay here," said Mattie. "If they're not on the level and they see him, that could be bad."

"Fair enough," said Giovani. "Actually, I think I'll find a quiet spot and get some rest." He exited the room.

Sister Catherine took charge. "Okay. Sister Margaret, Mattie, Trevor, and Tillie, you'll escort McEntire and only McEntire to Room 101, just down the hall. The others can wait outside. I'll grab Sister Timothy Ann and Cardinal Neubacher, and we'll meet you there in just a few minutes."

As the group moved through the atrium toward the front door, Tillie found her arm being snagged by Trevor, holding her back.

"You're really okay with this?" he demanded. "With actually drugging a man to give us information?"

Tillie shook her arm free, scowling fiercely at him. "Look, Trevor, whether you like it or not, we are now embroiled in a war–"

"Oh, whether I like it or not? Are you going to take any responsibility for this, Tillie?" Trevor's eyes narrowed. "I never asked for any of this."

"Really?" she scoffed, desperately trying to drown out the guilty little voice in her head that agreed with him wholeheartedly. "I didn't ask you to come after me when I ran off. In fact, I ran away to prevent you from getting caught up in this."

He looked like she'd punched him in the gut. "How could you ever think I wouldn't come after you?" he whispered. "It's been you and me our whole lives. Or at least that's what I thought. Until I found out about this secret life of magic you've been leading for fifteen years without me."

He was right, but– She swallowed and lifted her chin. "Well, you weren't hard to fool. Maybe I just figured since you'd been so easy to bluff for so long, you'd just bumble around for a couple of weeks and then give up."

Tillie spun on her heel and ran after the others without looking back, instant regret filling her entire being.

14.

Mattie finished guiding a bespelled McEntire into the atrium. The glow of her hands pulsed as the building's heavy front door slammed shut and she released the stasis spell on the two men she'd left outside, leaving McEntire frozen.

"Where the fuck are Trevor and Tillie?" asked Sister Margaret. Her swords were drawn and ready in case he managed to free himself from stasis. "They're supposed to be helping here. We could really use Trevor here to stitch this bastard into the classroom."

"We don't know that they're bastards," Mattie pointed out, but she wondered the same thing. "He's still levitated. I can just keep pushing him along. It's not far."

Just then, Tillie rushed out of the chapel, Trevor following at a more sedate pace.

Mattie looked from Tillie to Trevor and back again. Something had clearly happened, but she didn't have time right now to find out why Tillie looked like she was about to burst into tears and Trevor's face was frozen in icy fury.

"Trevor," she called. "Can you stitch him into—"

Before she could finish, Trevor strode over to McEntire, grabbing his shoulder and stitching both of them out.

"Well, okay, then," said Sister Margaret. She marched toward the classroom. Mattie followed closely behind her.

When they arrived in Room 101 a few seconds later, Trevor and McEntire were standing at the head of the room.

Trevor pulled the wooden chair out from behind the teacher's desk, and Mattie relaxed the stasis spell enough to assist McEntire into a seated position on the chair.

Sister Catherine entered the room, Sister Timothy Ann and Cardinal Neubacher just behind her.

Sister Timothy Ann bustled forward, laying out the syringe, cotton balls, and medical tape on the sturdy wooden desk beside McEntire's chair. "I'll need the stasis spell released completely for this to work; spells like that often slow down the heart, which makes the blood flow more slowly."

"Sure." Mattie put up a cage spell around McEntire and then released the stasis spell.

He shook himself out with a good-natured grin. "Damn, that spell is uncomfortable!"

"Sorry," said Mattie. "Unless you turn out to be a scumbag. Then I'm not."

"That's fair," McEntire laughed.

"You understand what they're planning here?" asked Trevor abruptly. "You don't have to do this."

McEntire looked surprised. "It's a truth serum, right? It's fine. I have nothing to hide."

"That's not the point," said Trevor. "You can refuse, go your own way. That's fine."

"I think that's really decent of you," said McEntire. He studied Trevor, his expression puzzled. "I don't know that I'd give someone the same option in your place. This is the world we live in, and it's generally not as kind as you are."

Trevor turned around, putting his back to McEntire – and Mattie couldn't help but notice that his back was also to Tillie, who had crossed to the far side of the room – and closed his eyes, breathing deeply.

When he opened his eyes, they locked with Mattie's and she saw in his face the same inner turmoil she'd been feeling before Ida's death.

Ida's words echoed in her mind. *I'm going to tell you a secret, dear. I hate killing. I hate battle and wars and combat of any kind. But I've been a warrior all my life. The secret is that I would never go into battle with anyone who wanted to kill. I will only fight on the side of people like you.*

Mattie gave Trevor a small smile, hoping it said everything she needed to say about how sick she felt inside, how off-balance she was, how everything had changed so quickly and she was just trying to move forward and do the right thing, but she didn't think she'd ever have Ida Garaveldi's moral compass.

Trevor's face softened as his lips curved ever so slightly in the saddest smile Mattie had ever seen. He understood.

Tillie couldn't see Trevor's face, but she watched the tension in his back ease somewhat as he and Mattie exchanged glances.

She suddenly felt very alone. Why had she said those terrible things to Trevor, especially when she'd already been feeling like he was pulling away from her?

Then again, he hadn't been in the world of magery for very long. He'd learn that it was too complicated to worry about things like this. Sometimes you had to make tough decisions.

Still, she regretted standing by for the decision to use the truth serum, and she regretted her harsh words to Trevor.

Hopefully she'd have a chance to make it up to him soon. For now, other things were happening.

She turned her attention to Sister Timothy Ann, who was now gesturing for Mattie to drop the cage spell so she could inject the newcomer with the truth serum.

Sister Margaret drew her swords, ready in case McEntire tried anything once the cage spell was down.

Mattie's hands stopped glowing and the faint bars of energy that surrounded McEntire disappeared.

Sister Timothy Ann hesitated for an instant, waiting to see if McEntire would make any kind of move, but he just smiled blandly at her.

She moved in and injected him with the serum, taping a cotton ball to the injection site afterward.

Mattie's hands began to glow again, and the cage spell went back up.

It had only taken a few minutes for the serum to go into effect when they'd used it on Madeleine.

Tillie slid herself into a hard plastic seat, folding her arms on the small square of desk connected to it, and leaned forward to wait.

Mattie picked up a student desk, turning it around so she could hop up onto the particle-board desk portion of it and put her feet on the chair. She propped up her chin on her hands, elbows to knees, and waited for the drug to take effect.

"How long does it take?" she asked.

"Not long at all," said Sister Tim. "On test subjects it's been anywhere from about ninety seconds to five minutes. We'll know it's working when he – ope, there he goes."

Mattie straightened her back, watching as the man began to sway slightly, his eyes going glassy.

Sister Timothy Ann gestured toward Cardinal Neubacher, and he stepped forward. "What is your name?" he asked, his voice gentle in an odd juxtaposition to his stern face.

"Ford McEntire," was the response. So, at least he hadn't lied about the most basic part of it. He really was Giovani's old partner.

"What is your purpose in coming here?"

"We hoped to get help against a team of agents from the organization known as the Auditors, who are hunting us. We also intend to offer alliance in the war against the Auditors in future battles."

"Who are you to offer an alliance?" Cardinal Neubacher demanded. "What is your role in our own organization?"

Ford shook his head. "I'm nobody. Just joined up a few months ago. But I know the higher-ups were interested. I heard them talking. And Lansdowne knows more. He's outside. He's the one you really want; he only had me do the talking because I know Garaveldi. Used to be partners, you know."

Sister Margaret caught Mattie's eye and jerked her head toward the door.

Reluctantly, Mattie jumped down from her perch. She really wanted to hear more of this. She hurried out to the front door to fetch the other two guys.

Arriving at the door, she hit the speaker button. "Okay, guys, we're ready for you."

They'd been facing away from her, and they jumped at her voice, spinning around, hands up and glowing.

Mattie grinned. "Don't try any funny business. I'm gonna freeze you and bring you into the interrogation room where we've got your buddy." Technically, it was an interrogation room, since an interrogation was happening in it. They didn't need to know yet that it was just a basic classroom.

The two men moved their hands into the universal sign of surrender, the glow dissipating as they dropped the spells they had ready.

Mattie hit the button again. "Appreciate you showing your willingness, but the stasis spell is uncomfortable enough as it is. You might not want to keep your arms raised."

They exchanged startled glances and lowered their hands.

Mattie let loose her stasis spell and opened the door, levitating them a few inches off the ground, and pushing them toward the classroom, one hand on the small of each back.

When she arrived in the classroom, Sister Margaret pointed her toward the far front corner of the room, so she deposited them there. She put a couple of chair-desks beside them and then erected another cage spell, releasing the stasis and levitation.

They shook themselves off and then sat down, quietly watching with interest as their compatriot's inquisition continued.

"How did you know to come here?" Cardinal Neubacher was asking.

"The Harpers have a constant watch on the Auditors," McEntire replied.

The what? What had she missed? Was the Harpers the name of their organization? Mattie supposed it was just about as idiotic a name as the Auditors, but what was up with these secret mage societies?

"We have scryers watching various factions as well as any courtiers we can access. We had a watch on Agent Miller, and then switched to scrying on Agent Poe once Miller was taken out."

Mattie sat up straight and her eyes widened. They'd been watching everything?

"We can't alwys see into this building," he continued. "But we noticed Poe was coming in and out of here pretty frequently, so we figured it was important."

"What do you know about the Order of Saint Joan?" asked Cardinal Neubacher.

Mattie frowned. Who cared? She wished he would get back to this whole constantly-scrying thing. She'd shared a house with Nicole Poe for a couple of weeks. Had they been watching her too?

Then again, Sister Margaret looked very interested in that question. Mattie couldn't help but notice that her friend was leaning forward, her shoulders tense and her jaw clenched.

"Nothing," said McEntire. "I mean, from context, I would guess it's something to do with the nuns here. But I've never heard of it before now."

Sister Margaret's jaw relaxed, but her shoulders didn't. "I want to hear from this Lansdowne character," she interrupted. "This guy clearly doesn't know shit."

Lansdowne stood up with no hesitation. "Certainly. I'm happy to submit to your truth serum and your questions, and am fully authorized to negotiate on behalf of The Harpers and our council."

Mattie looked at Trevor, whose face showed a certain amount of relief. She felt the same way. It appeared that all of these people felt perfectly fine about the truth serum, and while they probably had residual trauma out the ass from their time with the Auditors, this wasn't a trigger.

Making up the words as she went along, Mattie formed a spell in her mind to merge the two cages. The two spells elongated until they met in the middle, like a hallway of glowing gold bars. Lansdowne and the other guy – Freeman, was it? – helped McEntire to his feet and supported him down the length of the cage, helping him sit down.

Then Freeman took his own seat again, and Lansdowne went back to replace McEntire on the wooden teacher's chair.

A few minutes later, Lansdowne was clearly feeling the influence of the mage-spiked drug, and Cardinal Neubacher got to work.

"What is your name?"

"Lawrence Michael Lansdowne. I went by Mike when I was younger, then Agent Lansdowne when I was an Auditor agent. Now I go by Lansdowne."

"What is your mission here?"

"Escaping the team of Auditors who came after us, and negotiating an alliance with your group to help take down the organization."

"What is the mission of the Harpers?"

"To help agents who have escaped the Auditors hide from them."

Mattie was surprised. Their group had no interest in taking down the organization?

Apparently Cardinal Neubacher felt the same.

"Just to hide?"

"Historically, yes," said Lansdowne. "Your campaign has given us hope that maybe we could help take them down. We had intended to make contact at some point, but our hand was forced by the team coming after us on our supply run."

"What do you know about the Order of Saint Joan?"

"Nothing."

Out of the corner of her eye, Mattie noticed Sister Margaret relax.

Cardinal Neubacher continued. "When you say you were hoping to form an alliance, who exactly were you hoping to negotiate with?"

Lansdowne paused. "I'd like to answer the question, but I'm not sure I understand it."

Mattie cocked her head. It seemed pretty straightforward, although she wasn't sure why it was being asked. They wanted to form an alliance with the group taking down the Auditors organization, right? That included her and Tillie and Trevor and all of those former Auditor agents and the nuns and priests who were helping them.

The room was quiet as Cardinal Neubacher frowned, apparently pondering how to reword his query to clarify. "You asked to speak with Nicole Poe, correct?"

"Yes. Nicole Poe is the leader of the group of former Auditor agents who planned a rebellion against the organization. We were hoping to form an alliance with that group."

Their group really needed a name. Just not as dorky a name as the Harpers or the Auditors.

"Were you also hoping to form any kind of alliance with the Catholic Church or the Order of Saint Joan?" asked Cardinal Neubacher.

Lansdowne frowned. "I just thought a few nuns and priests had volunteered to help out with the battle and then maybe had allowed the group to use this convent as a base. They're connected with someone related to Agent Garaveldi, right?"

Ida had gotten the nuns and priests involved.

That answer must have satisfied Cardinal Neubacher, because he gave Lansdowne a small smile and a nod and moved on. "How many members of your organization came with you here today?"

"Just the three of us. Me, Freeman, and McEntire."

"How many members does your organization have altogether?"

"About two thousand."

Holy crap. Mattie almost fell off the desk she was sitting on. Glancing around the room, she saw that Tillie and Trevor looked just as startled as she was. Sister Margaret and Sister Timothy Ann just looked thoughtful.

Freeman looked slightly smug, and McEntire still looked stoned out of his gourd.

Lansdowne kept talking. "Some of those are escaped agents, some are court who have defected, and some are the families and descendents of older members, who have grown up as part of our group. We've been around for about five hundred years."

Tillie stifled a yawn. These interrogations were interesting, but she had missed out on too much sleep lately, and it was starting to catch up with her.

She was feeling less tense, seeing how casual these Harpers had been about taking the truth serum.

Mattie and Trevor were looking shocked again, but really, it only made sense that they'd been around for a long time, if their numbers were so large. How many newly escaped Auditor agents did they think there could possibly be?

Then again, this was another aspect of the two of them being so new to magery – they weren't used to the way that these societies lasted for centuries. Look at the Auditors; they'd been around since the Middle Ages.

She found her eyelids drooping and laid her head down on the desk in front of her.

A hand on her shoulder jerked Tillie back up.

Oh, no.

She must have fallen asleep. That was embarrassing.

As she lifted her head, she discreetly wiped her mouth with the back of her hand as she stifled another yawn.

The room was completely empty, except for her and Trevor. Tillie wondered if the Harpers had been taken into custody or released and were being treated as allies now.

She glanced up at Trevor, who was still standing beside her.

He quirked an eyebrow in that familiar way of his, and a rush of relief filled her. Maybe she hadn't ruined everything.

"Don't worry," Trevor said. "You didn't snore."

"Thank goodness for that," she muttered. "What did I miss?"

"We've tentatively decided to trust them," said Trevor. "Cardinal Neubacher determined that they were telling the truth about why they're here, who they are, and what they're all about."

"Did they question the other guy?" she asked. She pulled herself to her feet and stretched luxuriantly, lengthening her entire body upward, her hands together above her head in a full yogic mountain pose.

"Freeman?" Trevor shook his head. "I guess they figured since McEntire and Lansdowne gave pretty much the same answers, and it sounds like Freeman is almost as low-ranking as McEntire, there wasn't a reason to question him. The three of them are in the infirmary in the convent now, waiting for the drugs to wear off."

"Any sign of the Auditor agents who were chasing after them?" Tillie asked.

"Not yet," said Trevor. "I guess we'll have to wait and see if they track them here."

Just then, a faint, familiar buzzing sound came from the hallway.

Tillie frowned. "Is that the front door again?" She glanced at the clock situated above the blackboard at the head of the classroom. Six-thirty in the morning. "I feel like that can't be good."

Trevor's face was grim as he jerked his head toward the door. "Let's go see."

15.

Mattie gave her twin bed a wistful look. She would so love to just get right back in it and catch up on her sleep. She had always been an eight-hours-a-night, keep-sleeping-until-done-and-damn-the-consequences kind of person; one of the few traits she shared with her sister – other than the identical looks, of course.

She smirked. At least she had managed to stay awake through the interrogation sessions. Then again, it seemed like Tillie was losing out on even more sleep than she was.

Mattie resolved to find time for a real nap later, and to make sure Tillie did the same. Trevor and Tillie were determined to look after her? She could play that game too.

But right now, sleeping wasn't in the cards. Mattie pulled off her comfy jeans and t-shirt and changed her underwear. Then, with a sigh, she opened up the middle drawer of her dresser and took out a pair of form-fitting brown leather pants. Why was this becoming her new aesthetic?

She had to admit, as she put them on, that they were a lot more comfortable than they looked. She'd always thought leather armor would be stiff and itchy. Well, maybe *always thought* was a bit of a stretch. She hadn't thought much about leather armor at all until about a month and a half ago.

And she hadn't thought she would ever have to wear it until she'd started training with Sister Margaret and the nun had coaxed her into a set.

It was actually pretty soft against her skin and it moved well with her. And she'd found that it turned bladed weapons aside nicely.

Mattie spared a moment to wonder why mages were all about knives and swords. Why no firearms? She'd have to ask Sister Margaret.

Looking down at herself, Mattie was surprised to realize that as her mind had wandered, she had donned the rest of the armor and automatically distributed knives all about her person. Even now, her hands were busy with the last step – buckling on her sword belt, which held twin short swords, similar to Sister Margaret's.

She wasn't as good as the warrior nun with them yet, and probably never would be, but considering she'd only been using them for a few weeks, she could do some real damage.

She was better with magery, though.

Mattie picked up a black hair tie from atop her plain pine wood dresser, pulled her long hair back in a high, tight ponytail, and was ready to go.

Time to attend her first ever negotiation of wartime alliance.

What an odd feeling – two months ago, she'd been an ordinary high school English teacher. Now she was striding down the hallway of a convent toward a mage war summit.

The war room was just down the hall and around the corner from her bedroom, and she had never been in there. It turned out to be a very official-looking room dominated by a big, heavy wooden table lined with swivel chairs.

Only a couple of people were present, including Nicole Poe, her former housemate and the leader of the rebel agents they'd already teamed up with. She took a seat beside Nicole, who blinked at her and yawned.

Mattie laughed. "I think that about sums it up."

"Why does it always feel like these things have to happen in the middle of the night or the asscrack of dawn?" Nicole said with a wry grin. "I mean, the organization brainwashed us and stuff, but at least they let us get adequate sleep. Maybe I should consider just going back."

"They might take you," said Mattie. "But they wouldn't take me, so you wouldn't get to hang out with me anymore."

"Yeah, that's a dealbreaker," said Nicole. "So. There's a whole crapload of former agents out there who managed to break free, huh? And here I thought I was special."

Mattie nodded. "They've just been hiding out for hundreds of years."

Nicole frowned. "They're immortal somehow?"

"No, not the same guys," said Mattie. She sat up straighter, her eyes widening. "Wait, is immortality a thing?"

"Not that I know of," said Nicole with a shrug. "Seems unlikely. Probably impossible, in fact. I think witches might live longer than other people? But witches can't be mages. They're the only people who can't."

"I've heard mention of witches," said Mattie. "What's the deal with them?"

"I don't really know much about them," said Nicole. "They hate mages. For some reason mages are supposed to hate them too, but I don't really know why. Maybe someone who grew up in a mage family would know."

As though on cue, Giovani ambled into the room, taking a seat across the table from Mattie and Nicole.

"What do you know about witches?" Mattie asked.

He shrugged. "Very little. Why?"

"Are they regular people?" said Nicole. "They're not immortal, are they?"

His eyebrows shot up. "Not that I know of. I've never heard of actual immortals. Outside of fiction, I mean." He nodded toward the door as it opened mechanically and a black-clad figure in a wheelchair rolled in, one pant leg tied in a knot about where a knee would usually be. "I know Father Sean has had run-ins with witches. Maybe he can tell you more."

Mattie frowned. Father Sean usually used a prosthetic leg. "Are you okay?" she called toward him as he positioned his chair at the end of the table.

He gave her a tired smile. "Just tired. It's easier on my body to use the chair when life gets a bit busy like this."

"Are you sure you don't want to sit this one out?" asked Nicole. "Not that we're not always glad to have your help, but–"

"I am sitting," he said, sharply. "Nothing wrong with my mind; I'm happy to help strategize and negotiate."

"Of course," said Nicole, but her face remained troubled, her posture tense.

Mattie wondered if the leadership role was getting to her. It couldn't be easy to be in a position where people died because of orders you gave, and it was surely demoralizing to have so many people leaving your command in a short space of time, cracking under the pressure.

"We were just talking about witches," Mattie said. "Giovani suggested you might know something about them."

Father Sean huffed, a humorless laugh. "You might say that. Witches both made my career and cost me my leg. There's not a lot I can tell you about them, you being laypeople, you know, but I'm happy to answer any questions that don't violate any of my oaths."

"Are they immortal?" asked Nicole.

Father Sean looked wary. "Witches? No. Their lifespan is quite similar to ours."

The way he said it made Mattie think he was talking about a different species; were witches not humans?

"Barring accidents or disease, they tend to live anywhere from ninety to a hundred and twenty years," he continued.

A hundred and twenty years? Mattie sat up straighter in her chair. Maybe they weren't humans. What else was out there, then?

Just then, a crowd of nuns trooped in, led by Sister Margaret, chattering loudly and taking seats all along the table.

Sister Margaret plopped into the chair next to Father Sean and gave him a broad grin. "You sure you're up for this, old man?"

He snorted. "Old I may be, but don't count me out just yet."

She leaned back in her chair, her booted feet swinging up onto the table. "I would never presume." Sister Margaret pulled a small knife out of her left boot and began cleaning her fingernails with it idly as she looked around. "Are we all here?"

"The guests of honor appear to be missing," observed Sister Catherine. She gave Sister Margaret's feet a pointed look.

Sister Margaret's smile widened as she pulled her feet down and straightened her posture. She took a whetstone out of one of the many pockets of her bandolier and started sharpening her dagger.

"I believe Sister Beatrice is bringing the Harpers' representatives shortly from the infirmary," said Sister Regina. She adjusted her whimple, but it was still crooked.

Very shortly, apparently. Right on Sister Regina's words, Sister Beatrice, a tiny, shrunken elderly woman with dark skin and sharp brown eyes, led the three men into the room.

The Harpers were still wearing their suits, but they were rumpled and looked sort of . . . hungover. Which made sense, now that Mattie thought about it; they'd been drugged and then given just enough time for the drugs to wear off before being brought in.

"How do you feel?" asked Sister Tim with the intensity of a scientist gathering data. Her pen hovered above a notebook.

"Not great," said McEntire, his cheerful tone belying the words.

Lansdowne was less cheerful as he added. "Sort of like a giant cat has been batting my head around, but refusing to kill it."

Sister Timothy Ann wrote that down and then looked expectantly at the last Chameleon, who was cradling his head in his hands and staring at the table. "And you, Mr . . . " she consulted her page. "Freeman? How are you feeling?"

Freeman looked up, his brows furrowed. "Well, I didn't take the drugs," he said.

"I know," said Sister Tim. "But you somehow sort of look like you did."

He shook his head. "I'm sorry. I'm just tired. We've been going and going for a while today – well, yesterday actually – and I just really need some sleep."

Sister Margaret stood up. "Then let's get this party started so you boys can get some shut-eye."

"Wait," said Mattie, looking around. "Where are Tillie and Trevor? They should be here, right?"

Sister Margaret glanced at the clock above the door. "We can't wait. Trevor knew the timeline and said he'd pass it along to Tillie. If he didn't do so, or if they were delayed, then that's on them."

Sister Catherine stood as well. "If you don't mind, Sister, I would like to direct this meeting."

Sister Margaret nodded and sat down.

Lifting her arms, Sister Catherine continued. "Thank you all for coming. This is an auspicious moment for our little movement, as we gain allies against this deadly enemy. As many of you know, the Church as a whole is a bit busy right now–"

A ripple of grim laughter went through the room, and Mattie exchanged puzzled glances with Giovani, Nicole, and Bernie.

"–leaving our little bastion of warrior mages to finish what we started almost entirely on our own," Sister Catherine finished.

"I think we can handle it," said Sister Margaret, swiping her blade across the whetstone with a flourish and a bloodthirsty grin.

A few of the other nuns cheered.

"Nevertheless," said Sister Catherine, "we are pleased to welcome a new group of allies to the table."

McEntire nodded an acknowledgement. "We, in turn, are gratified to find other groups willing to stand up to the Auditors, and look forward to taking more definitive action against the organization, having spent so many centuries merely hiding from them."

"I know these diplomatic meetings can tend to drag on," said Sister Catherine, "but I think we can all agree to condense the niceties this once, and move on to negotiations so that Freeman here can take a nap."

This time, Mattie joined in the laughter.

"We are prepared to offer sanctuary to these three men," Sister Catherine gestured to the Chameleons seated across from her. "We can also offer our convent as a safe house for your organization going forward, on an as-needed basis."

McEntire's spine straightened and his brows rose. "That's very generous," he said, cautiously.

Sister Catherine gave him a tight smile. "Much as I would love to use that perceived generosity as a bargaining chip, I feel ethically bound to disclose that it's actually part of the mission of our order," she said gently. "We offer sanctuary and protection to the oppressed."

McEntire nodded, his face thoughtful. "Thank you for your honesty," he said.

"And now we get to the meat of the deal," she went on. "This is not part of our oaths. We are prepared to assist you in tracking down and disabling the Auditor agents who are after you three right now." She paused, as though waiting for McEntire to speak, but he just nodded. "In exchange for which, we ask for full rights to any Auditors we can take prisoner in the process."

"May I ask for what purpose?" said McEntire.

Mattie thought that was kind of a stupid question. Obviously, the nuns wanted to interrogate them, just like they had the Harpers, and Shezza – she was having trouble thinking of her as *Madeleine*.

She was having trouble thinking of Shezza as an ally too, although everyone else seemed to think she suddenly was.

Mattie wondered if Shezza now thought of herself as an ally. Did she even remember what she'd said during her time under the influence of the truth serum?

If she was such an ally now, why wasn't she here in this meeting?

And speaking of missing people, where the hell were Tillie and Trevor, anyway?

Tillie opened her eyes groggily. She was seated in a crooked slump, leaning against a hard surface. Straightening her back, she felt her entire torso twinge in protest of her position.

Where the hell was she? Hadn't she just woken up in the classroom a few minutes ago?

Oh, right. The doorbell. She and Trevor had gone to answer the doorbell. Who had been at the door? She couldn't remember.

Tillie scrambled to her feet and looked around. She was in a strange cube-like room with no door. She stretched out her arms and could graze each side with her fingertips.

Taking a single step forward put her in the center of the room, and she spun slowly around, arms still outstretched, gauging the size. It must have been a perfect square.

The ceiling wasn't much higher either; straightening to her full height put her head about an inch away from it.

Gradually, she began to notice a sound as well, like a huge machine was running nearby. Once she identified the sound as an engine, she realized the air smelled faintly of exhaust.

And where was Trevor? Trevor had been with her at the door; she was sure of it. Who had been on the other side of the door? She couldn't even remember getting to the door.

The last thing she could recall was the bell ringing. Trevor had just woken her up and they were the only people in the room.

They had gone out into the foyer, and Trevor was telling her that everyone else was already heading to the convent for a formal negotiation meeting.

She couldn't remember reaching the foyer. Who had been at the door?

She gasped and stumbled as the room jerked suddenly and then began to move. Leaning against the wall again, Tillie struggled to catch her bearings.

A train. She must be on a train. There was something bad about being on a train, wasn't there? Something Giovani had said once about–

Tillie slapped her hands over her mouth, stifling the impulse to let out a horrified scream.

The Auditors. When they took you, they put you on a train.

16.

Mattie pulled her phone out of a pocket in her leather bandolier as she left the war room. Sister Catherine had made good on her promise to keep the negotiations brief, and it seemed that the Harpers were just as eager to come to a quick agreement.

They had agreed to the terms of turning over the prisoners, and then had offered a high number of soldiers in the upcoming battles, and the nuns had accepted.

Giovani and Nicole, as representatives of the non-religious types, had also agreed to the terms, and Mattie had volunteered for the task force assigned to turning the tables on the agents hunting the three Harpers.

Said task force, led by Sister Margaret, had decided to embark upon their mission after everyone had the opportunity to rest up, so Mattie was heading to her room to finally catch up on her shut-eye.

First, however, she texted Tillie. *Where the hell are you? You missed the whole meeting.*

No response had come in by the time she reached her room. She frowned at her phone.

Better try Trevor too. *Where are you guys? Are you okay?*

Mattie hesitated as she reached for the buckle on her bandolier. No sense in getting ready to go back to bed if she was just going to have to armor up again if her sister and friend were in trouble.

A text came in, and she snatched her phone up off the bed where she'd tossed it.

It was not Tillie. It was her stupid ex-husband – well, technically still her actual husband as their divorce hearing was still coming up. When was that thing again? She expanded the text to read it. *Are you coming home for our hearing at least? It's next fucking week, you know.*

She rolled her eyes. Like she had time for something as ridiculous as a divorce hearing. *Fuck it,* she typed in. *You can keep everything. Just fax me the papers and I'll sign them.*

She fumbled through her purse, knowing she had a business card the St. Elizabeth Academy receptionist had given her, with all the contact info for the school. Finding it, she typed in the fax number and hit send.

A wave of relief washed over her, and she realized just how stressed she had been in the back of her mind about this upcoming hearing. "Should have done that weeks ago," she muttered.

Another text came in from Craig. *Fine. Expect it later today.*

She grinned and sat down on the bed. Her phone dinged again and she held it up, hoping for Tillie or Trevor this time.

Mattie groaned. Craig again. Why? *I'm still worried about you. I wish you'd tell me what's going on. Why you're still out there and why you left everything behind.*

She thought about it for a moment. It was kind of sweet that he was concerned. Then again, he had never been that concerned about what was going on in her life while they'd been married.

He was always just running off to hang out with his friends with no regard for her work schedule or her needs. Just constantly making plans without her, and if she complained, telling her that she was welcome to join him, knowing full well that she had to work in the morning and couldn't be showing up all groggy, or worse – hungover.

She scowled fiercely. *Mind your own business. We're done here.*

Mattie scrolled up to the texts she had sent to Tillie and Trevor, her scowl fading into a worried frown. It had been a good five minutes since she'd texted Tillie.

That was very unlike Tillie, and she knew that she had her phone on her. The last time Tillie hadn't been answering texts, it was because she was on the run from the Auditors.

Tillie slid her back down the wall, bending her knees and ending in a crouch. She bunched her hands in her short red hair, massaging her scalp and breathing deeply to calm herself.

Closing her eyes, she straightened her back and folded her legs into a lotus, seating herself on the floor and taking long breaths in and long breaths out.

She was going to be okay.

The reason the Auditors put new "recruits" on a train was to disorient them, take them to a new city where they would be less likely to be able to escape.

Tillie refused to be disoriented. She was no ordinary kidnapee this time. She knew the organization. Well, she knew them more than most outsiders did, anyway.

And she had allies on the outside who knew about them too.

Her eyes flew open. She might just have an ally inside with her, in fact. Had they gotten Trevor? Was he on the train with her?

Time to tally up her assets. Tillie patted down her pockets, but they were predictably empty. Whoever had taken her would have cleared them of anything useful, and Tillie never carried anything that wasn't useful.

Next, she looked at her feet and realized they had taken her shoes too. Damn. That was unfortunate, but she still had – nope. They had removed her bra as well, which felt a little invasive and creepy, honestly. But she had to admit it was very astute, since she had a few small but handy things hidden in every bra she owned.

Finally, she ran her hand along the waistband of her linen pants, probing the tiny pockets she had hidden underneath each belt loop, her smile widening as she pulled out item after item.

A tiny dagger, the blade just two inches long. A spare key to her condo. A folded $100 bill. A little plastic vial that held three ibuprofen. A bundle of bandaids. A slim packet of protein powder. A skinny obelisk of clear quartz that could be used for scrying in a pinch. And, last but very definitely not least, a beacon-spelled amulet given her by a friend that could be activated without magic.

Since she was absolutely sure they would have blocked her mage abilities, this was invaluable. Granted, the friend in question had no idea that the Auditors existed, so she didn't know how much help she could possibly be.

But it couldn't hurt to activate it anyway, right?

Tillie set the amulet on the floor in front of her and positioned her finger right above it. She picked up the dagger and poked the fleshy pad of her finger, wincing as it went through the skin.

Dropping the dagger, she massaged the finger with her other hand until a drop of blood welled up and hit the amulet.

Then she carefully wiped her finger clean on the hem of her shirt – wishing she'd thought to include a sterilizing pad along with the bandaids – and covered up the small wound.

Mattie called Tillie, and the call went straight to voicemail without ringing. Something was very wrong. Tillie never turned her phone off, and she never let the battery die.

She called Trevor and his phone was off too.

The next call she made was to Sister Margaret. As soon as the nun answered, she got straight to the point. "Tillie and Trevor are in trouble."

"What? Mattie, I just fell asleep. We don't have time for this." Sister Margaret sounded groggy. Apparently she wasn't a magical non-sleeping automaton after all.

"I'm sorry. But this is serious." She explained about the phones as she headed down the hallway toward the high school and the classroom she had last seen them in.

"Okay, fair enough," said Sister Margaret. "I'll meet up with you in a few minutes."

Mattie hung up without saying goodbye, striding through the foyer of the school. She was about to turn left toward the classrooms, when she noticed something odd outside, through the glass double doors. It looked like – was that somebody's foot, peeking out from behind the bushes?

She approached cautiously and crouched down to peer out. There was a white sneaker, positioned toe-down, like someone was lying on their stomach just beyond the shrubbery. Reaching for the door handle, she hesitated.

It could be a trap. It was most likely a trap.

Mattie turned on her seer sight and the future showed her finding exactly what she thought she'd find – a person stretched out, unconscious, on the lawn.

The person was a young man who looked vaguely familiar, but she couldn't place him.

It didn't look like a trap in her future vision, so she pulled open the door and walked out, seer sight still going.

She knelt beside the prone figure and gently turned him over, studying his face in the present, while keeping an eye on the immediate future for any signs of an ambush.

Still not quite recognizing him, she reached for his throat to check his pulse. It jumped beneath her fingers, so she put him in a stasis spell and levitated him to bring him inside.

It seemed like that was her most frequently used combination of spells. She smiled grimly. Maybe she could start a super sketchy business with that.

Got enemies? We'll freeze 'em and get 'em into your basement dungeon for you! Just $500 a pop!

What could go wrong?

"Oh, crap," she muttered, as she watched herself in the next few seconds realizing that she hadn't propped the door open with anything.

Turning off her seer sight, Mattie stepped back up to the door and cupped her eyes with her hands, trying to see if anyone was in sight. If she was lucky, Sister Margaret hadn't come through yet, and she'd be able to let her in.

Her luck held and she pounded on the door as Sister Margaret came into view.

Sister Margaret's long black braid swung around as she spun toward the door, drawing her swords as she turned, and then she relaxed as Mattie gave her an exaggerated shrug and a wry smile.

The nun sheathed her swords and hurried toward her.

"What's up?" asked Sister Margaret as she opened the door. "Who the hell is this?"

"I'm not sure. I can't quite place him," said Mattie. "I found him lying on the grass outside. He looks familiar, though, right?"

Sister Margaret studied the young man, who was very well-groomed, neatly dressed, and handsome in a kind of skinny, elfish way. She snapped her fingers. "He was at that battle, wasn't he? In the Auditor building."

"On our side?" asked Mattie. She looked closely at the guy's face. "Oh, yeah. He's that kid who just wandered in, right? He thought it was a roleplaying game or something, and got partnered with Tillie and Trevor."

"He's not a mage?" said Sister Margaret with a frown. "What is he doing here?"

"I have a better question," said Mattie, grimly. "What does his being here have to do with Tillie and Trevor disappearing?"

Just then, her phone began to ring. She pulled it out of her bandolier and looked at the screen. "I don't recognize this number." Mattie silenced it and was about to put it away again, when Sister Margaret reached out and grabbed her hand.

"Answer it. Maybe Tillie or Trevor managed to find a payphone or something."

Mattie raised her eyebrows. "In the 21st century?" She swiped upward on the phone, however, and hit the speaker button so Sister Margaret could hear too. "Hello?"

"Uh, hi," said a nervous, feminine voice at the other end. The voice was too high to be Tillie's. "Is this Mattie Holiday? Tillie's sister?"

Mattie's eyes met Sister Margaret's. "Yeah, this is Mattie," she said.

"This is Stephanie Bing. We met at your sister's funeral. I was a friend of hers."

"Right." Mattie nodded. "You own that magic shop in the Central West End."

"Magpie Magic, yes." The woman paused. "What I'm going to tell you might come as a shock." She paused again.

Mattie wished she would get on with it. They had missing persons to deal with and an international secret society to bring down.

"I think your sister is alive."

Sister Margaret made an impatient face and rolled her hands around each other in a clear *get to the point* gesture.

Mattie grinned at her and waved at her to stop. "Yeah, we're actually aware of that," she said to Stephanie. "She is, however, missing again, so any information you have would be extremely helpful."

There was a long pause, and finally Sister Margaret muttered, "Oh, for fuck's sake," and leaned toward the phone, speaking into the microphone. "Hola, Stephanie. My name is Sister Margaret and I'm also a friend of Tillie's. May I ask what prompted you to make this call this morning?"

"Hi, Sister Margaret," said Stephanie finally. "We've actually met before. You're at St. Elizabeth's right?"

"Yes, I am," said Sister Margaret. She made a strangling motion toward the phone. "Do you have any information about Tillie's whereabouts?"

Mattie pressed her lips together to keep from laughing at Sister Margaret's exasperated antics.

"Actually, I might," said Stephanie. "I gave her a bunch of beacon amulets a while back, for her birthday. She was really excited about them and said she was going to put them in her emergency pockets in all her favorite outfits. You know how Tillie was . . . is, I guess? Always insane about keeping one step ahead of everyone else. Anyway, I spelled these so that it could only be activated by her blood."

"That sounds sort of unsanitary," Mattie muttered.

"It's standard," said Sister Margaret with a shrug.

"Yes," said Stephanie, a little bit of pique in her voice. "And it's a good thing I did, because she activated one of them a few minutes ago, and if I hadn't set it to be blood-activated, I would have assumed that someone else set it off by mistake, and I wouldn't have called you."

"Fair enough," said Mattie. "Sorry. So, what exactly does this beacon amulet do?"

"It tracks her location," said Stephanie, "and sends it to an app on my phone."

"How very modern," said Mattie. "You're the one who told Trevor that secret societies are passe and nobody pays them any attention anymore, aren't you?"

"They are, and nobody does," Stephanie snapped. "Why? Are you one of those ridiculous Knights-Templar-wannabes? Dressing up in robes and prancing about, thinking it gives you more power, when all you really need is some damn practice? Or maybe you just don't have the capacity to do the really strong magery."

"No," said Mattie. "I agree with you on that point. I just wish the secret society that keeps kidnapping people did too."

Stephanie paused again before continuing. "Well, anyway, I have Tillie's location. She's actually moving very quickly away from St. Louis, heading north through Illinois."

"Toward Chicago, maybe," murmured Sister Margaret. "Do we think Trevor is with her?"

"That I couldn't tell you," said Stephanie.

"Is there any way we could get a link to see what you're seeing?" asked Mattie.

"No," said Stephanie. "I take the security of these amulets very seriously. I have this app programmed to be unshareable. I can keep you posted, though. Text you every so often with updates."

"That would be great," said Sister Margaret. "Thanks for calling. Adios." She reached over and hung up Mattie's phone.

"Well, that was abrupt," said Mattie.

"We don't have time for chit chat," said Sister Margaret. "You heard her. Tillie is moving very quickly away from St. Louis."

"So, what? We jump in a car and head for Chicago?" said Mattie. "I just need to grab–"

"No, no, no," said Sister Margaret. "We can't do that. We have a task force here. We have to help these Harper people and find the agents hunting them."

"Oh, right." Mattie had forgotten about the Harpers in all the excitement. She glanced at the college kid who was still levitating in stasis beside her. She released the stasis spell and gently lowered him to the ground.

He sat up immediately and looked around frantically. "Where am I? Did they get her?" he yelped. "What the fuck is happening?"

17.

Tillie paced the tiny room, leaning against the wall to keep her balance as the train rushed toward wherever the hell it was going in such a hurry. She ran her hands over the cool metal walls, searching for any kind of opening.

It was probably futile. Why would they bother to put a door in the cell when they could just stitch her in? And once she was in, her own magery was stifled, so she couldn't stitch herself out again. It was the ultimate in security, and she was honestly surprised the nuns of the Order of Saint Joan hadn't thought of it.

Then again, she remembered, when Shezza had kidnapped her and handed her over to Nicole, there had been spells preventing her from spelling and seeing, but not stitching.

Experimentally, Tillie moved her fingers in a simple gesture, trying to move herself across the room. Nothing happened. The cells on these trains were probably much more secure than the HQ cells, since the train itself wouldn't be as secure. Plus, Nicole hadn't been acting on behalf of the actual Auditor organization, and hadn't been following proper protocol. Maybe didn't even know how to follow protocol, since she was a station agent and not a field agent.

Or was there another kind of agent who handled the transport and imprisonment of the newly kidnapped mages?

Too bad she hadn't had the energy to read the rest of those books they'd gotten yesterday. There had been one about the hierarchy of the organization that would have probably been really helpful.

She waved these speculations away. Pointless to reminisce about the past or on what she didn't know. She needed to focus on what to do now and how to prepare for whatever would come next.

She couldn't escape from this cell at the moment. No problem. She'd just have to escape from the next place they took her. And she would have to figure out a way to bring Trevor along too.

It would help to know where Trevor was. Maybe he was in an adjoining cell. How big could these Auditor transport trains be, after all, if they were riding the rails incognito?

She braced her left hand against the wall and began rapping her right knuckles sharply against the hard surface, tapping out a staccato message in Morse code. *Hello,* she tapped. *Do you know me?*

It was a code she and Trevor had laughingly discussed, years ago on a tipsy evening spent seated beside the fire pit in his backyard, that they would use to identify each other in times of duress.

She smiled at the memory.

"We need a code, in case one of us is kidnapped," Trevor had insisted. "Something we can say on the phone so the kidnappers won't know it's a code, but we will."

"Why would we be kidnapped?" she'd asked.

"I mean, we probably won't, but we definitely will if we don't have a code," had been his logic. "You know things are less likely to happen if you prepare for them to happen."

"Well, that's true," she'd conceded.

So, they'd come up with *Do you know me?* as a sort of stilted but not unusual question that might not get the kidnappers too confused.

And then they'd figured that the person on the other end of the phone wouldn't have to worry about anyone overhearing, so they would say the countercode of *pineapple, turquoise, scissors,* and the kidnapped person would just say, "Yes," if they had been kidnapped, as though the other person had said something completely normal, and then the other person would come to the rescue.

Since there wasn't really a need for subtlety in this situation, she began tapping out the other three words too.

Once she'd finished, she waited for a response, but none came. So, he wasn't on the other side of that wall.

Tillie stepped carefully along the wall, keeping one hand on the metal to maintain her balance in the swaying train, until she came to the corner and moved into the center of the next side. And then she began to tap again.

"Did who get who?" Sister Margaret demanded.

At the same time, Mattie asked, "Where's Tillie? Did you see what happened?"

"Tillie, yes," said the kid. He clutched his head and moaned. "It's kind of fuzzy. I think they did that magic stuff on me."

"Who?" said Sister Margaret. "What kind of magic?"

He stared at her, confusion written across his face. "What kind?" he repeated.

"He doesn't know anything about magery," Mattie pointed out. "What's your name again?"

"Sammy," he said. "And I've been learning. Well, trying to anyway. I have a lot on my plate right now. Taking some summer classes to try and graduate early, you know."

"Okay, Sammy." Mattie put an arm around his shoulders and guided him firmly toward a group of chairs off to the side of the foyer. "Let's sit down. You've had a rough morning, haven't you?"

"I have!" he said, sinking into a chair. "I think I'm still a little drunk from last night."

Ah, youth. Mattie remembered those days. Sort of. She remembered that they'd happened anyway. The details were a little fuzzy.

She sat down beside him. "Okay, so why don't you start at the beginning."

Sister Margaret sat down across from them and looked pointedly at her wrist, even though there was no watch there.

Mattie frowned and Sister Margaret rolled her eyes. "Actually, let's start as close to the end as you can and still make sense," the impatient nun suggested.

That was fair.

"Okay," said Sammy. "So, I was leaving the bar, just over on South Grand," he waved toward the commercial district that was just a couple of blocks away, "and these four people were sort of clustered in a group just down the street a little. They caught my eye because they were dressed like, well, like how you two are dressed." He paused. "No offense."

"None taken," said Mattie.

"And I figured they had to be mages, because that's how a lot of the people on our side at that crazy fight were dressed. You know the one right before you all trashed my apartment, which I never got any kind of compensation for, by the way."

"You saved the lives of a lot of people by letting us use your apartment to funnel everyone out of the burning building," Mattie pointed out.

"I think 'let' is a strong word," he retorted. "But fair enough. We can talk more about that later. Anyway, I told my friends to go on to the next spot without me, and I snuck over to listen to the mages talking."

"And they caught you," said Sister Margaret, flatly. "That was a dumb move, kid."

He shrugged. "Might have been. Nothing I can do about it now. Yeah, they caught me, and they asked me a bunch of questions, which I refused to answer because I'm not a snitch. And then they, like, tied my arms down to my sides with magic, so I couldn't move them, and there was some other magic where I couldn't talk, or at least no sound came out when I did talk, and they shoved me in the trunk of this beat-up old car, which really stunk, like I think the last person they put in there threw up and they didn't really clean it up right. It was bad."

"Get to the point," Sister Margaret growled.

"Right." Sammy was starting to perk up a little. Clearly he was someone who enjoyed being the center of attention. "So, what happened next was kind of weird."

Mattie raised her eyebrows. He didn't think the part he'd just told them about was weird?

"They drove me here and I was just sort of lying in the trunk for a long time, like probably hours – I fell asleep. I woke up when the trunk opened all on its own, or well, probably with magic, right? And then I realized I could move my arms again, so I climbed out. The mages were nowhere to be seen, but when I tried to run away, I couldn't go in any direction except up the front path to this building. Every time I tried, I hit a wall. So, I came up to the building and rang the bell."

"What time was this?" asked Sister Margaret. "I didn't hear the bell ring."

"It had to have been after we left the classroom," said Mattie. "We wouldn't have heard it in the convent, right?"

"I'm not sure," said Sammy. He tapped the step counter on his wrist and it lit up. "I didn't think to check. Wow, it's already almost eight. I have class in like an hour."

"I don't think that's going to happen," said Sister Margaret. "Get back to your story, please."

"Yeah, well, I can't miss my 11:30, anyway," he said. "So, I rang the bell, right, and then Tillie came up, with that hot guy she was with that other time too; what's his name?"

"Trevor," said Mattie. "He's ace, so don't get any ideas."

"Right, he said that before. A boy can look, though, right? Anyway so, they came up and Tillie was talking to me through the intercom and I asked if I could come in, and she was about to buzz me in, but Trevor said it could be a trap, and I was like, 'He's got a point; maybe I should just try and go away,' and then she was like, 'what do you mean try?' and I told her the whole story, and then I felt something hit me in the head, and next thing I knew I was in here and you guys were on the phone and I couldn't move and then suddenly I could move and here we are."

"Sounds like the agents were hoping she would open the door for him and then they got impatient," said Sister Margaret.

"She must have tried to help Sammy when they attacked him again," said Mattie. "Or Trevor did. Trevor never could let a bully win."

"Good for him," said Sister Margaret. "I mean, in this case, it didn't end up being good for him, but it's just generally a good policy to fight off bullies. I'd have done the same. But I would have actually fought them off and not gotten myself kidnapped."

"Do we think these are the same agents who were after the Harpers?" asked Mattie.

"Good question," said Sister Margaret, thoughtfully. She pulled out her phone and typed out a swift text message. "Sister Helen took a statement from them, including a physical description. Shouldn't be too much trouble to compare notes with this one."

Her phone dinged and she typed in a brief response.

"Okay," said Sister Margaret. "Off to a good start – there were four agents in both cases."

"Two teams, I guess," said Mattie. "Since they usually work in pairs."

Sister Margaret nodded. "Makes sense, since they had multiple targets." She turned to Sammy. "Okay, so can you describe the four who attacked you?"

He nodded. "It was three men and one woman. They were wearing the same kind of weird leather gear you have on, like I said. The woman was blonde and short. One of the guys was Black and had these super soulful eyes and you could tell he was fucking ripped. They all had killer bods, in fact, but the other two were kind of wiry, you know? While this guy was all muscle." Sammy smirked. "In fact, he was the one who grabbed me, and he was holding me kind of tight against his abs, and I will tell you right now, I didn't mind it so much, you know, until he threw me in the stinky trunk."

He paused and Mattie and Sister Margaret just stared at him.

His smile faded. "Anyway. There was an Asian guy with a super intense face, like you could definitely see him being in, like, a badass kung fu movie, unless that's racist, but either way, he was smoking hot too, and his leather just really clung to his body in all the right spots, you know?"

Mattie's lips twitched and she glanced over at Sister Margaret who also seemed to be holding in laughter.

"And the last guy?" said Sister Margaret in a strangled voice.

"White guy. Really fantastic, classic face – chiseled jawline, high cheekbones, the whole Prince Charming package. Kind of short, but I don't mind that, generally, and he had kind of longish wavy brown hair that looked really soft, like I just really wanted to run my hands through it."

"And the woman . . . ?" said Sister Margaret.

Sammy shrugged. "I told you. Blonde and short."

Mattie chuckled. "I mean, at least he noticed *something* about her."

Sister Margaret grinned. "Fair enough. And it does sound like this is the same group. I mean, the descriptions I have here are worded very differently, but the gist is the same."

Her laugh fading, Mattie considered this. "So, do we think they are all heading northward with Tillie and Trevor, then, or did they split up?"

"Or did they put Tillie and Trevor on a train and stick around to finish up the job they started?" suggested Sister Margaret, her voice grim.

"Oh, that's right. It's trains, isn't it?" said Mattie, thoughtfully. "I used to take the train a lot when I was in college. Chicago is a big hub. If they get them to Chicago, there are tracks going in all directions from there. They could end up anywhere."

"We better try to head them off there then," said Sister Margaret. "This needs to take priority. Let's see what Sister Catherine wants to do about it. My inclination is to go haring off immediately into the great north, but it needs to be her call. We still have an obligation to the Harpers to help them, at least if we want their help in this war."

Sister Margaret was typing in a text to her superior before Mattie could say anything, so she just shrugged. No matter what Sister Catherine said, Mattie knew she'd be going after Tillie and Trevor. There were plenty of other people around who could help the Harpers.

Besides, it sounded like the two missions were pretty much the same.

Tillie faced the final wall. This was it – her last hope that Trevor was in an adjacent cell. She breathed in deeply and then exhaled with a whoosh.

And then she began to tap. *Hello. Do you know me? Pineapple, turquo–*

She stopped. Someone was tapping back! She counted the taps, and began to laugh. *Scissors,* came back at her. "Yes!" she yelled.

Tillie started tapping again. *I think we're on a train. The Auditors have us. Do you remember what happened?*

Yes, came the response. *Auditors. You don't remember?*

Somehow, Tillie could hear the concern in the tone of Trevor's taps. *Doesn't matter,* she tapped back. *Need a plan. I set off a beacon spell. Stephanie might be able to find us.*

Stephanie thinks you're dead, tapped Trevor. *Will she respond?*

Crap. She hadn't considered that. Tillie closed her eyes. Why had they ever thought that faking her death would be a good idea? It had been such a spur-of-the-moment plan. Damn Mattie and her speller ways.

That wasn't fair, though, especially since Mattie had changed in just the few short weeks she'd been practicing magery – all kinds of magery. And it actually had been a good plan, and it would have worked, if only they hadn't killed Agent Miller in the process.

If only they'd known who Agent Miller was, and that she was really on their side. Sort of.

Tillie forced her attention back to Trevor, who was tapping again. *They have to let us out sometime. We wait. Then attack and escape.*

Tillie nodded. It was really the only thing they could do. *Glad we're together this time,* she tapped back.

There was a pause, and then Trevor tapped, *Me too, love.*

Maybe their friendship would survive this after all.

18.

Sister Catherine was still in the war room, talking quietly with Bernie, who was showing her something on a laptop computer.

"Does it say anything on your message board about Tillie and Trevor?" asked Mattie.

Bernie shook his head. "I don't think so, but it's hard to tell. Of course, this forum is about clandestine operations – spy stuff. Not about the Auditors' ordinary business of kidnapping morphers."

"Yeah, but Tillie and Trevor aren't ordinary morphers," Sister Catherine pointed out. "It does seem like the board would be full of chatter about this war, right?"

Bernie nodded, but his brow was furrowed. "It does seem that way." He ducked his head down, rubbing the back of his neck with both hands. "The problem is that this code is so simple, and yet so obnoxiously difficult to make heads or tails of it."

"So, let's bring in the expert," Sister Margaret suggested.

Bernie shrugged. "Sister Helen and her crew are doing the best they–"

"Not the linguistics expert," said Sister Margaret, shaking her head. "The one who has used this board herself. Where's Madeleine?"

Sister Catherine frowned. "She's still in the infirmary, recuperating from the truth serum."

"Well, if the Harpers were well enough for a war negotiation, then why isn't she well enough for this?" said Mattie. "If anything, she went first, so she's had more time for the drugs to wear off."

Sister Catherine hesitated. "Madeleine is a whole different case," she said slowly. "She really needs to be handled delicately or we could lose her as an ally."

"Well, my sister needs to be found, or we could lose her as a living person," Mattie snapped.

"That is certainly a consideration," said Sister Catherine. She sighed. "All right. But we talk to her in the infirmary, not here."

"Fine," said Mattie.

"And you must speak to her with kindness," said Sister Catherine.

Mattie paused and considered this. "I'll do my best."

Bernie stood up. "Well, I'm out." He gestured toward his computer, which still sat on the table. "You can use Bessie to show her the forum, but I don't think I'm ready to confront the woman who killed my wife, no matter how brainwashed she has been."

Sister Catherine laid a hand on Bernie's arm. "That's fair. Get some rest."

He nodded curtly, pulled his arm free, and strode out of the room.

Sister Catherine stood as well and gestured toward the door. "Shall we?"

The infirmary wasn't far, as and they walked, Mattie did her best to put herself into a frame of mind in which Shezza – no, Madeleine – was a good person who was on their side.

Of course, they didn't know she was a good person. As far as Mattie could tell, the only thing that had really come out of the interrogation was that Shezza – Madeleine – was traumatized. Trauma didn't necessarily make someone a good person.

It might give them an excuse for bad actions, but it didn't mean that they weren't bad altogether, and it certainly didn't mean that they would immediately start doing good things, just because they were away from their abusers.

Mattie thought the nuns were being uncharacteristically naive about this whole thing. But she needed Shezza's – dammit, Madeleine's! – help to get Tillie and Trevor back, amd if that meant playing nice with the crafty bitch, then so be it.

As they reached the infirmary door, Mattie squared her shoulders and muttered, "Madeleine. Her name is Madeleine. Madeleine, Madeleine, Madeleine."

Sister Margaret smirked at her. "You got it?"

"I think so. Let's do this."

The infirmary was a large room that smelled like rubbing alcohol and antiseptic ointment. It was divided into three sections, each of which contained five hospital beds with curtains in between.

On one end of the room, the three Harpers were fast asleep on their beds.

At the other end, Madeleine reclined on a bed, her torso propped up a little bit, reading a book.

Sister Beatrice sat on the bed next to her, also reading a book, but somehow conveying an air of alertness.

If Sister Beatrice was supposed to be a guard, that seemed like an odd choice to Mattie. The woman was eighty if she was a day.

Then again, she would have trusted Ida with the task, and Ida had been just as old.

Come to think of it, Sister Beatrice was an excellent choice if the goal was to post a guard without giving the impression of posting a guard. Assuming she was as capable as Ida had been of kicking some ass in her old age.

As they approached the pair, Sister Beatrice put her book down and gave them a cheerful smile. "Come to visit our guest, have you?" she said.

Sister Catherine returned the smile. "If she's up to it."

Madeleine finally lowered her own book. "Depends on what you're looking for from me," she said, warily.

"We just want to talk," said Sister Margaret.

Madeleine eyed Sister Margaret's swords and raked her gaze over the rest of her person as well, her eyes pausing minutely in spots where Mattie knew the nun hid various weaponry.

Mattie had no doubt that Madeleine was ferreting out every single dagger, hatchet, and throwing star in just a few seconds.

"Yes," said Madeleine. "You do seem to have come prepared for a light chat."

Sister Margaret shrugged, her lips twisting into a wry smile. "This is just my default. I'm sure you can relate to that."

Madeleine met her eyes and her own lips twitched slightly. "I can, actually."

Mattie stepped forward. "Tillie and Trevor are missing. What do you know about it?"

Turning her head to study Mattie, Madeleine's eyes narrowed and her smile faded. "I've been here for hours. I was drugged before that, and languishing in a very secure cell before that. What do you think I know about it?"

"You were roaming around the building causing who knows what kind of havoc before that," Mattie retorted. "I think you know a lot, and I want to know it too."

Sister Catherine lifted her arms. "Enough. Mattie, you promised to be nice."

"Yeah, Mattie," said Madeleine with a smirk. "Can't you be nice for once?"

"As for you–" Sister Catherine turned toward Madeleine. "–we are glad you're here and happy to give you sanctuary from the Auditor organization. But we have some rules, and those include being civil to those who live here."

Madeleine bowed her head in acknowledgement. "My apologies, Sister. You're right, of course. I misspoke."

Mattie crossed her arms over her chest. She wasn't buying this suddenly meek persona. She'd seen how easily Madeleine switched up her personality.

Sister Catherine set down Bernie's laptop on the small table beside Madeleine's bed, and opened it up.

"Wait!" said Mattie. "Sister, can I talk to you in private for a moment?"

Sister Catherine tipped her head to the side and studied Mattie for a second before nodding. She gave Madeleine a warm smile and then stepped toward the door to the infirmary.

Mattie followed. "Do you really think it's a good idea to show her that we've hacked into that forum?" she asked, once they were out of earshot. "She could still be reporting back to the court somehow."

Sister Catherine sighed. "At some point, we'll have to start trusting her. I'm inclined to do so now. And after all, that same forum mentions her as missing."

"Sure," said Mattie. "But that was before we let her out of her cell. Now that she has some freedom, she might be able to get a message to them."

Sister Margaret strode over to them. "What are we chattering about over here?"

"Do you think we should be trusting her with the information that we've managed to hack into the court's dark net stuff?" Mattie demanded.

Sister Margaret shrugged. "Maybe not. If we can't trust her, this is a great way to find out. This is a relatively small victory; not a huge deal if they block us out or stop using the message board, but if they do, then we'll know she ratted us out."

Mattie nodded slowly. "That's a good point."

"Good, so we're decided." Sister Margaret pivoted on her heel and walked back to Madeleine's bedside.

She grabbed the open laptop, clicked a couple of times, and then swiveled it to face Madeleine.

Madeleine's eyebrows shot up. "You must have some kind of tech wiz on your team, huh? Meerkat did this site, and even Raccoon couldn't break in when she tried."

"Meerkat? Raccoon?" Mattie sat down on the other bed, beside Sister Beatrice. "Where do you come up with these code names?"

"Well," said Madeleine absently, her attention still focused on the computer screen. "Meerkats live in elaborate underground burrows, and our Meerkat is brilliant at keeping our organization underground, keeping things hidden, etcetera.

Raccoons are known for their abilities to break into shit. As is our Raccoon."

"And chameleons are known for blending into their surroundings, and you change personalities like most people change socks," said Mattie.

Madeleine glanced up, giving her a small, tight smile. "Exactly." She looked back down at the computer and her face lit up in a larger grin. "Here we go. 'Nosotros perdimos a los músicos.'"

"Músicos?" said Sister Margaret. "Do they mean the Harpers?"

"Yes," said Madeleine. "It's a code we often use for the Order of Harpocrates."

"Oh," said Mattie. "Of course. God of secrets. That makes sense. I wondered what a harp had to do with anything."

"There's more here, though," said Madeleine. "'Hemos tomado una nueva misión de transporte. Dos zorros.' Foxes are the code we've designated for your group. So, this means the team was hunting Harpers and has abandoned that mission in favor of transporting two of your number."

"Foxes," said Mattie. "That's not too bad. I've been thinking our group needs a name."

"Anything else about where they are or where they're going?" asked Sister Catherine.

Madeleine shook her head. "They'd be on a train, of course. And my best guess is that they'd be headed to Utah, to Broken Bunker Station."

"Utah?" Mattie frowned. That sounded a little out of the blue. Something tugged at the edge of her mind, though. Something someone had said about Utah…. "Amy," she said aloud. "Amy mentioned some kind of station she was at in

Utah, where the books were off-limits and everything was kind of weirdly secretive."

"Yep," said Madeleine. "That's Broken Bunker." She took a deep breath and closed her eyes.

Mattie and the others watched her in silence. She seemed to be wrestling with a big decision. What was so important about Broken Bunker?

Madeleine finally opened her eyes, her face pale. "Broken Bunker," she said, slowly, "is the world headquarters of the Auditor organization, since the early twentieth century, when they moved it from their original castle outside of Brussels." She took another deep breath. "That's where you will probably find my father."

19.

Tillie studied the tray of food that had just appeared in front of her. To eat or not to eat. That was the question.

She was disappointed but not surprised that they had stitched in just the tray of food and not brought it in person.

The food looked good. It consisted of a submarine sandwich with meat and veggies on a hearty wheat roll, accompanied by a small bowl of coleslaw and a glass of water.

On the one hand, it was important to keep one's strength up. On the other hand, there was a good chance it was drugged. She wished once again that she could use her seer sight and see just what would happen after she ate the food.

A tapping began on the wall beside her and she turned her attention toward it. *Do you think we should eat?* asked Trevor. He must have gotten a tray at the same time as her.

I don't think so, she tapped back. Better to be safe, right? She was very hungry, though.

Agreed, he tapped back.

Damn. She had been half hoping he would disagree, and then she'd have an excuse to eat. She hadn't eaten in hours.

Tillie pushed the tray away from her and resolutely turned her head away from it, settling back down to wait once again.

Mattie opened the door to Giovani's SUV and hopped into the front passenger seat. As she buckled her seatbelt, Giovani got into the driver's seat and Nicole, Amy, and Sister Margaret piled into the back.

Sister Catherine had argued that they should bring Madeleine along, but before Mattie could strenuously object, to her surprise, Madeleine herself pointed out that she would be dividing their team. Until Mattie could trust her, her presence would be a liability splitting Mattie's focus between the actual objective and watching her like a hawk.

Mattie was now torn between thinking it was awesome that Madeleine would make that point, and also thinking that it was just what she'd say to win Mattie's trust if she was still just fucking with them.

How did they even know that she was telling the truth about how important this bunker was? Or that the train would definitely be going up to Chicago first and then heading west? It seemed very out of the way; why wouldn't they head toward Kansas City instead, if they needed to go through a major city?

Mattie twisted around to address Amy. "You're sure Broken Bunker is the name of the station you were at before?"

Amy raised her eyebrows from the middle seat. "Yes, Mattie. For the twelfth time. Broken Bunker is the weird underground station in the middle of nowhere Utah where I was stationed. And yes, Mattie, for the twelfth time, Broken Bunker is where the books were all spelled so I couldn't look at them and the place we stole those books from yesterday.. And yes, Mattie, for the twelfth time, it's the one where the security was all crazy high." Amy's voice was uncharacteristically tart.

Fair enough. Mattie sighed and turned back around. "Something just seems fishy."

"Look," said Giovani, pulling the car out of the parking lot. "It's good to be cautious. We absolutely shouldn't be taking everything Madeleine says at face value. I agree. But the fact is that we have to rescue Tillie and Trevor before they get to a station, and this is the only lead we have. Stephanie has eyes on the beacon amulet's signal. She says it's still heading north, right?"

Mattie checked her phone. True to her word, Stephanie had been texting every fifteen minutes or so to confirm that the little red dot that was Tillie was still heading north. "Yeah."

"So, we go north."

Tillie woke up with a start. She had no idea how long she'd been asleep, but the tray of food was gone. She tapped on the wall.

Fell asleep. Any news?

She waited, but no response came. Trevor must be napping as well.

Tillie felt her eyelids drooping again. She might as well get some more rest. She needed to be alert for whatever was coming, but she didn't need to be alert right now.

Mattie woke up to find herself slumped against the car door. "Where are we?" she muttered, sleepily.

Only Sister Margaret was still sleeping, her quiet, rhythmic snores providing an odd counterpoint to Giovani's classical music.

"Almost there," said Giovani.

Mattie checked her phone, studying the screenshot Stephanie had sent her just a few minutes ago. "Tillie's still pretty far from Chicago – looks like she's just a little north of

Bloomington. You guys were right about the train making frequent stops to avoid detection."

"Do you know where Chicago has its waystation?" asked Nicole. "We should head them off there."

Giovani frowned. "The what?" he said.

"The waystation. You know, where they stop the trains so they don't have to go to the main stations?"

"Huh. I never knew about that," said Giovani.

"That, right there, is why this whole thing is so hard," Mattie sighed. "Not only do we know hardly anything about the organization, but even the people within it only knew a small portion about it."

Nicole's lips twisted in a grimace. "You're not wrong. Amy? Do you know?"

"I want to say Joliet," said Amy. "I think Bernie would know for sure."

"I'll give him a call," said Nicole, pulling out her phone and fiddling with it for a second before holding it up to her ear. "Hey. Chicago's waystation. Where is it? . . . Joliet? Great. Perfect." She hung up and told Giovani, "Amy's right. Head toward Joliet, if you see a sign. I'll figure out where we're going from there."

She began typing into her phone, but continued talking to the rest of them. "So, what happens at the waystation will depend on whether they're actually bringing them to Chicago for processing or just passing through. Either way, they'll probably stop here, since it's one of the bigger stations and they'll typically want to fuel up and stretch their legs. But if they're not moving on, they'll take the new recruits off the train and move them into a van. They'll be drugged and unconscious, so be prepared for that. And we'll have to fight off the team bringing them in and the two station agents at the waystation. It'll be a short window while they transfer the recruits from the train to the van. Then the transporting agents will drive off immediately while the station agents take control of the train.

"On the other hand, if they're just stopping for refueling and a little break, Tillie and Trevor will stay on the train and we can jump aboard while the agents are busy, break out the recruits, and sneak off with little issue. That's the scenario I'm hoping for. I think they'll be a little more complacent and we'd have more time."

"Plus it sounds like Tillie and Trevor would be able to help once they're free," said Amy.

"Got it!" Nicole waved her cell phone triumphantly. "They're calling it the Actuary Depot. I have directions now." She hit a button and a tinny voice emerged, instructing them to continue on the interstate for another three and a half miles and informing them that they would reach their destination in twenty-three minutes and that they were on the fastest route.

Mattie twisted around to peer into the back seat. "Somebody better wake up the sleeping nun."

Tillie woke up again as the train slowed down again. This train made more stops than a bus. It was getting ridiculous. She jumped to her feet to stretch out while it was stopped.

She hoped there would be some action soon – she felt well-rested and ready the break the hell out.

The train only paused for a minute, and then it started back up again, and suddenly it was going much faster than it had before.

Maybe they were making up for lost time.

As the car pulled into the small, run-down parking lot in front of a small, run-down shack by the railroad tracks, Mattie got another text from Stephanie. "You guys, she's moving faster, and she's still heading our way. Her dot is right next to the Joliet dot."

Giovani parked in one of the three spots, beside a black windowless van. It had no markings on it, and looked like any other van – the kind of vehicle your eyes would just slide over.

Mattie got out of the car with the others and stretched her limbs. They had driven straight here from St. Louis, taking the typically-five-hour drive in about three and a half. But that was still a lot of sitting.

The door of the shack opened, and she tensed up. They'd agreed that Nicole and Giovani would do most of the talking, but it would look weird if she refused to speak. Hopefully the station agents wouldn't say anything to her.

"Afternoon, agents . . . ?" said the woman who emerged from the waystation.

"Jones," said Nicole. They had no way of knowing if their actual names had been circulated throughout the organization. "And I've got Agents Matts, Joseph, and Lopez here. We're on special assignment, heading to Chicago. Orders are to wait here for a train coming in from St. Louis."

"Right," said the station agent. "I'm aware of the train. Wasn't told about your team. Come on in, and I'll message HQ. I'm sure we'll get this all sorted out."

Mattie saw Nicole's shoulders stiffen. So much for the hope that the station agent would just take their word on it.

Time for Plan B.

She readied a spell as the Auditor turned back toward the shack.

Her spell was rendered unnecessary a moment later, when Sister Margaret, in one smooth motion, pulled a dagger from her sleeve and threw it with deadly accuracy at the agent's throat, slicing clear through it.

"One down," said Sister Margaret, retrieving her knife. She wiped it clean on a brown handkerchief and resheathed it, stowing the hanky in a pocket of her bandolier.

"There will be another station agent," said Nicole. "Best to take them out quickly before they realize they're alone."

"Too late," said Mattie, nodding her head toward the single window of the shack, where she could see a pale face studying the scene.

The man in the window locked eyes with her and a cruel smile blossomed on his face as he drew a finger across his throat in a way that she supposed he imagined was intimidating.

It really just came across as cheesy.

Without a second thought – or any ridiculous posing – Mattie threw a fireball at the window. The force of it broke the glass and she threw another one directly after it. The second one hit a shield and fizzled out.

"Shields up," said Giovani. "He's a speller."

Mattie put up her own shields and extended them to cover Sister Margaret, since she was the only one who didn't spell in their group.

She belatedly moved her eyes into seer mode as well.

"Abomination!" yelled the man inside the shack, as soon as she did so, because of course he did.

"Try minding your own business," called out Sister Margaret. "You might be happier. I know I would."

The man disappeared from the window and emerged from the shack a moment later, advancing upon the group, slightly blurry through the shield that surrounded him.

Through her seer sight, Mattie saw his plan to throw a lightning bolt at Nicole, and she stitched it away to hit the black van instead.

The man's eyes bulged in rage at her triple-threat abominating, and he began to mindlessly toss lightning bolts in her direction.

Pouring all of her mage strength into her shields, Mattie weathered the storm, holding his single-minded attention by widening her white-filled eyes and moving her fingers through a series of gestures. There was no stitching power behind the gestures, but since her hands were already glowing from the spells, she figured he wouldn't be able to tell.

While the Auditor hit her with spell after spell, Sister Margaret and Giovani inched unobtrusively around behind him. Nicole and Amy strode into the shack, where Mattie knew they would be busy sorting through information, looking for anything about the train they were here to meet.

Mattie lifted her arms dramatically to distract the agent, as Giovani began throwing spells at the back of his shields, trying to weaken them.

Suddenly, Mattie saw with horror a small chink in her own shield. Time seemed to slow down as she shifted her focus to desperately fix the hole, her attention lasering in on the tiny hole in the shimmering shield.

The glow around her hands pulsed again and again as she patched the hole each time the speller's lightning hit it.

And then a bolt got through. She saw it coming in her seer sight before it did and she realized she couldn't stop it.

Mattie twisted desperately so that the bolt hit her in the arm instead of her torso, howling in pain as the shock hit, just above her elbow.

Dropping to the ground, she saw through hazy vision as Sister Margaret punched through a hole in the Auditor's shield and pierced his heart.

Time still moved like molasses as she watched the man fall to his knees and then forward onto his face.

The last thing she saw before passing out from the pain was Sister Margaret running toward her and skidding to a halt by her side.

Tillie felt the train slowing down again and scrambled to her feet, leaning against the wall, ready for it to lurch to a stop. It had done this several times since she'd woken up, and each time she'd prepared for it to be really stopping, but this time, she could feel in her bones – or maybe in her suppressed seer abilities – that this time meant action.

Without turning around, she tapped on the wall behind her, *I think this is it.*

Let's kick some ass, came back from Trevor, and she grinned widely.

"Do let's," she murmured aloud.

Mattie woke up to find Amy bent over her, hands glowing and stitching.

Her arm still hurt, but it was no longer the blaze of agony it had been just a moment ago.

Giovani and Sister Margaret stood by, watching her closely.

Nicole ran out of the building, holding a black tablet. "The train should be here any minute, and it looks like they will be moving on, but it doesn't say what the final destination is."

An alarm began to clang nearby, and Mattie struggled to sit up, so she could look up the tracks. Beyond the bell and the flashing lights, she could see the oddest little train car heading their way.

It looked like a box on rails – like an ordinary freight car, except that it was moving, without the benefit of an engine car. She knew it must have a motor somewhere, or maybe it ran on magery somehow, but it was very disorienting to see something that shouldn't be able to move on its own doing so.

The car was slowing down as it approached.

"Oh, no, you don't," Amy admonished. "Let's get you back to the car. I've eased some of your pain, but stitching can't actually undo damage caused by a spell. You're out of this fight."

Mattie opened her mouth to protest, but then she caught sight of her arm, the skin blackened in spots, reddened and blistered in others, and the worst parts – yellow and bubbly.

She turned her head in the other direction, emptying her stomach onto the ground.

Moaning, Mattie wiped her mouth on the sleeve of her good arm as best she could.

"Ready?" said Amy.

Mattie nodded. She closed her eyes as Giovani's hands glowed and she felt herself levitate a few inches upward. So, this is what it felt like. At least no one had frozen her in place, but it was still very disorienting.

Someone – probably Amy – put their hand on the small of her back and gently pushed her along.

She opened her eyes and saw that they were just about to the SUV.

Amy stitched open the back door. She stopped and moved Mattie's floating body into a reclining position and guided her into the car, hovering over the back seat.

Giovani's spell changed and she was delicately lowered onto the seat.

Mattie gritted her teeth to keep from screaming as the impact – small as it was – jostled her injured arm. "Just breathe," she muttered to herself as the door slammed shut behind her head.

She forced her lungs to expand into a deep inhale and then shakily let it out.

"Again," she told herself. "Just keep breathing." This breath was a little bit easier. The next was easier still.

She could hear shouting from outside the car.

Mattie closed her eyes again, focusing on her breathing. She grasped the smooth flesh of her forearm just below the burnt area with her other hand, immobilizing the arm as best she could and then leveraged her legs to pry herself up into a seated position.

Clenching her teeth, she managed to keep herself from howling again.

Slowly, she twisted herself around to watch the fight through the window.

The train finally stopped and Tillie arranged her limbs into a ready krav maga stance, waiting for someone to come and try to remove her from the cell.

Then again, maybe it was better not to fight them. There was no way she could get out of the room without someone else stitching her out, since her magery was blocked by the Auditors' spell.

Tillie relaxed her stance, leaning against the wall again.

The minutes ticked by, and nobody came for her or stitched her out of the room.

Suddenly, the train car was rocked by an outside force, hitting it with a huge bang. Tillie staggered, struggling to catch her balance again.

As Mattie watched, she identified the four agents Sammy had described.

Ripped Black Guy was fighting Sister Margaret's double swords.

Chiseled-Jaw White Guy dodged concrete blocks from a slag heap stitched at his head by Amy, while she ducked under his broad strokes with an actual ren-faire-style mace. Mattie winced as one of the concrete slabs smashed into the side of the train.

Short and Blonde grappled hand-to-hand with Nicole, skillfully keeping the stitcher's hands busy as they fought, so Nicole couldn't do what Amy was doing.

And Wiry Asian Guy was retreating from Giovani's berserker morphing.

As Mattie watched, still breathing as slowly as she could, Giovani sliced his glowing hand sideways and Wiry Asian Guy fell, blood flowing from a wound in his side.

His shields must have failed.

Mattie managed a faint and ragged, "Hurrah," but it trailed off as the pain in her arm grew.

She closed her eyes and focused on her breathing again.

Tillie waited. If she listened closely, she could hear fighting going on outside the train. Every couple of minutes or so, another crashing impact forced her to cling to the wall or fall.

She moved her feet into a sturdier, bracing position.

And she waited.

The pain receded once again, and Mattie opened her eyes.

Giovani had joined Amy, and the tide had turned in their favor. Mattie watched as one of Amy's concrete blocks found its mark and smashed into his head.

Chiseled-Jaw White Guy went down.

Without missing a beat, Giovani and Amy split up, Amy joining in Sister Margaret's fight, and Giovani rushing to Nicole's side.

But the agents had other plans. Short and Blonde's hands glowed and a flare went up.

As soon as Ripped Black Guy saw it, they both began to retreat, moving away from their opponents and back toward the train.

Giovani's hands pulsed and a shimmering shield popped up in their path.

Ripped Black Guy turned slightly and stitched a concrete block back at them, hitting Giovani in the stomach.

"Noooooo!" shouted Mattie, as Giovani crumpled to the ground.

Giovani's shield flickered out and the two remaining Auditor agents pushed through to the train.

Amy and Nicole stopped and crouched beside Giovani, while Sister Margaret rushed after them, managing to stop Short and Blonde short of the door, engaging her with her swords.

Ripped Black Guy kept going, disappearing behind the train.

"No," Mattie whispered.

Sister Margaret slashed her swords across Short and Blonde's throat and turned toward the train car as the agent fell, but it was too late.

The car had begun to move.

Tillie looked around in confusion as the train lurched and began to move once again. She could have sworn she heard Mattie's and Giovani's voices coming from outside. And she'd been so sure this was their final stop.

What had gone wrong? She leaned against the wall and sank down again until her butt was on the floor and wrapped her arms around her upturned knees in front of her.

Next time, she'd just eat the damn sandwich.

20.

Mattie stitched herself into the very back of the SUV to make room for Giovani to lay down across the back, and stitched open all four doors, as Sister Margaret rushed toward her.

Nicole and Amy followed at a more sedate pace, and Mattie was relieved to see that Giovani was on his feet, levitated and being guided just as she had been.

He clutched at his abdomen, and Amy supported him with an arm around his waist, while Nicole steered.

"What's the plan now?" Mattie gasped out, as Sister Margaret reached the car.

"We need to regroup and get you and Giovani some medical attention," said Sister Margaret, her voice grim. "And of course they now know that we're coming, so who knows what they'll do with Tillie and Trevor."

"Actually," said Nicole, maneuvering Giovani into the SUV, "I believe they'll follow the same trajectory. We already thought they were taking them to Broken Bunker, right? And that's the most secure place they have?"

"Yeah," said Amy. "There's really no reason this would change that. If anything, it would confirm it."

"But we didn't head them off," said Mattie. She paused and took a deep breath before continuing. "So, yes, we knew they were taking them to a secure location, but the whole point was that we didn't want them to get there. Our mission failed."

Sister Margaret shrugged. "Sometimes you fail. Nobody died, so that's something of a win. Well," she amended smugly, "nobody on our side."

"Jury's still out on that," gasped Mattie as another wave of pain hit her. Whatever Amy had done before was either wearing off or had been negated by all of her moving around.

Amy peered back at her, moving her fingers in a stitch, and the pain disappeared completely. "Now that I can focus on you, I should be able to keep you stable until we can get to a medical facility."

Mattie realized that not only did her arm no longer hurt, it was also held completely immobile by Amy's magery. She sighed in relief.

Sister Margaret typed something into her phone. "My order has a convent here in Chicago, which should have basic medical facilities. We'll go there, see if they can patch you guys up. If nothing else, they can get you to a hospital, and the rest of us can head back out to try and liberate that train again."

Her phone dinged and she lifted it up to read it. "Mother Joanna is expecting us. Head toward downtown."

"Got it." Nicole sped across three lanes of traffic and cut someone off to get back on the interstate, amid honks and outstretched middle fingers from the surrounding cars.

Sister Margaret let out a stream of Spanish that just had to be nothing but curse words.

"What?" said Nicole. "I'm from Chicago. This is how we drive."

21.

Mattie sat on the infirmary bed, her right arm bandaged up, and gratefully ate the sandwich the nuns had given her. Between the excitement that morning with Shezza – Madeleine – and then the Harpers, and *then* rushing after Tillie and Trevor, she hadn't eaten a damn thing and hadn't even realized it.

She wasn't sure if it was a really delicious sandwich or if she was just absolutely starving, but either way, she was enjoying the hell out of the spicy rich meat covered in peppers and onions.

Giovani was on the next bed over, scarfing down his own food, his two broken ribs set and stitched back to healthy by one of the nuns.

Apparently, since his injury had been caused by the impact of the stitched concrete, and not by direct magery, it was easier to heal by magery.

Mattie looked up as Sister Margaret plopped down at her side and reached for one of her fries. She quickly swallowed her bite of sandwich. "So, what's the word?"

Sister Margaret shook her head. "They can't spare any warriors to help us out right now. This is a very busy convent; lots of crap happens in Chicago, plus there's the whole–" She stopped herself from saying something and finished, "Well, there's a lot going on right now."

"So, what's our next step, then?" asked Mattie. "Did they say anything to you about when I'll be up and ready to go?"

Nicole pulled up a chair in between their beds. "Turns out third degree burns are no joke. I'm sorry, Mattie, but I don't think you'll be able to come along."

Mattie stared at her. "Listen, if you think I'm going to stay here, while you–"

Sister Margaret took another fry out of Mattie's plate, and Mattie moved it further away from her with a slightly annoyed frown. "Look, Mattie, I know you want to help, but you'll be better off as a reserve; you can't fight without your dominant arm, for fuck's sake."

Mattie's phone dinged. It was a text from Stephanie. "Tillie's on the move again. Heading southwest."

"That checks out," said Amy, leaning over Nicole's chair to grab another fry from Mattie's plate.

"Okay, everyone needs to stop eating my food," said Mattie.

"You should have eaten it faster, then," said Nicole. "This is what happens when you're the last one with fries left."

Mattie rolled her eyes at her.

"So, we're heading to Utah, then," said Giovani.

"I'll be right behind you," Mattie vowed. She was just too tired to argue. Which meant they were probably right. A thought occurred to her. "Hey, I wonder if all my stuff is still in that guy's garage."

Also by Anna McCluskey

Mathilda Holiday
Magic Today
The Viper's Head
Hello, Darkness
Brick by Brick
Time's Up (coming Fall 2022)

Rhymes With Witch
A Curse, A Key, & A Corkscrew
Witches & Weed
Magic, Mayhem, & A Martini

About the Author

Anna McCluskey is an independent fantasy author known for her witty dialogue, whimsical storylines, and immersive style. Anna lives in rural Oregon with her husband and way too many pets and plants.

For information on upcoming projects, check out her website, www.annamccluskey.com.